The Perils of Being

PJ SCHRIEVER

ISBN: 1461087007
ISBN-13: 9781461087007

I would like to dedicate this book to my son,
Jaxon, for whom I continue to create and reach
wildly for the stars. And to my sister, Cat, who was
my tireless cheerleader and editor on this project.
Thank you for being there for me.

ℒ

During her fourth period daydream, Lucy noticed that the sky had turned dark outside. She blinked hard, pushed her glasses back over the bridge of her nose and peered out of her classroom window; night had fallen abruptly, even though it was technically daytime. Hovering above the tree-tops was an angelic looking girl with jeweled wings that twinkled in the moonlight.

Lucy squeezed her eyes shut again, doubting that she had actually seen what she thought she saw. But when she opened them, the winged girl was still there, floating amongst the stars. Lucy twisted around to see if any of her classmates had noticed that there was someone flying around outside.

No. It didn't appear that anyone had seen anything unusual besides Lucy.

The girl greeted Lucy with a smile. "I've been expecting you," she whispered.

This is strange, she thought and half-smiled back.

"I have a gift for you." The girl pushed her wavy hair aside and removed the sparkling pendant that hung around her neck.

Lucy stared at the necklace as it dangled from her fingertips.

"Take it," she said.

Enchanted by this otherworldly girl creature, Lucy reached her hand slowly toward the glittery gem, but as her fingers stretched out to accept this offering, her ink pen rolled off her desk and onto the floor, and the clack of plastic hitting wooden planks jolted Lucy back into reality.

She reached down, quickly grabbed the pen and looked outside again for the mysterious winged girl. The boy who sat behind Lucy snickered.

"Shoot!" The otherworldly girl was gone, and so was the night. Daylight had returned, proving that what she had just seen was nothing more than her imagination playing tricks on her. Lucy looked into the empty sky and sighed. All that remained was the pale white moon, lingering above the trees, despite the sun's appearance.

Lucy wondered if the girl were one of her own creations that had sprung from her mind and come to life outside her English class. She enjoyed conjuring up characters for her stories, but none had ever appeared so clearly or spoken directly to her before, like a real person who had a mind of her own.

Before she could forget what the girl had said to her, Lucy wrote, "*I have a gift for you,*" and made a note of the shiny pendant she had been offered. She closed her eyes and pictured the girl in her mind, hoping she could produce her return.

This will make a great story, she thought, and scribbled down a few more details to summarize what she had just witnessed: *Pale milky skin, lavender sparkly wings. Angel or Ghost?* No, neither, Lucy thought and scratched a line through both creature types, replacing it with *Unknown Origin*.

Lucy strummed her fingers lightly on her desk and pondered what to name her. Sophia, Isobel, or Victoria—none seemed to fit. She finally settled on *Violet*, on account of her purple-toned moonlit pallor.

The clunk of Mrs. Wheeler's sensible shoes approached, and her brown tweed skirt skimmed the edge of Lucy's desk. Lucy sat up attentively, turned to a clean page of her Language Arts notebook and wrote: *MY STORY*, as her teacher had instructed her to do. She slouched back into her chair when she heard the same overly cheerful voice say the words "true" and "autobiographical" as she further explained the writing assignment.

"YOU will be the main character in the drama of your life. This is not fiction! I want to know all about you," Mrs. Wheeler announced.

Dread overcame Lucy as she considered how humiliating it would be to tell her life story in full detail to her sixth grade homeroom. Her real life was a subject she wanted to keep private. There was no way that she would admit to the entire class that her dad had traded her family in for a new one over the summer break. It had all happened so fast. One day everything seemed normal, and the next, she learned that her parents were divorcing.

The family breakup seemed to be caused by the arrival of her father's "love child" with his new girlfriend; that's what her mom called the mystery baby. Lucy worried that her dad might have left because of the lie she told, which resulted in a big fat argument between them, but her mom assured her that there were other reasons, including this new baby "brother." Lucy hated this secret sibling for being born and ruining her life—the one that had been just fine before.

No, she did not want to meet him, not after all the trouble he had caused her family. He had taken her father away, and now they were alone in that rotting old house they lived in.

Lucy's mother insisted that the cottage she had inherited was "quaint and rustic," but it looked to Lucy like it was about to fall down around them. It creaked and leaked and everything was broken, just like their family. Her mom kept saying that everything was going to be okay, but Lucy knew she didn't really believe that. How could she, when she spent most nights sobbing and filling the recycling bin with empty wine bottles? Lucy knew this because one of her chores was to take out the trash.

I wish I had wings like Violet, Lucy thought. I'd fly far away from here.

The only person Lucy trusted with the details of her life was her friend Jax, who pinky swore not to tell anyone at school. Besides, how would her teacher know if she was telling the truth or not? Mrs. Wheeler didn't know how pathetic her life actually was. It wouldn't hurt to use a little imagination here and there and make boring Lucy a little more interesting.

After her teacher walked to the other side of the room, Lucy looked out the window again, hoping to see Violet. Violet's possibilities were endless.

The bell rang. It was time for lunch.

"This day is stupid," Lucy whispered. She leaned back against the rough brick wall of the lunchroom, removed her new red-framed glasses and stuffed them in her sweatshirt pocket.

Waiting in the lunch line, she felt invisible to her classmates as they talked excitedly about their summer vacations and their new clothes, which they obviously chose while shopping together. Lucy looked down the line for Jax, who she thought might be able to save her from feeling like she was on display as the weird friendless kid. But he did not appear.

As the girls jabbered on, Lucy couldn't help but think how much more exciting their lives seemed than hers. One of them finally acknowledged her and asked, "What did you do this summer?"

"I went to Crystal Lake," Lucy said. "I mean, when I got back from the rainforest. You know, the Amazon rainforest?"

She couldn't help but embellish the truth. The part about Crystal Lake was true. Lucy had spent many warm sunny days at the local swimming hole. But the closest she had gotten to any rainforest was when it drizzled in the woods that surrounded her house. The Amazon idea just popped into her mind, triggered by a travel commercial she had seen on TV yesterday. It was so much better than the truth.

The girls smiled politely and turned away from her to continue their discussion about their new shoes.

For Lucy, the only good thing about school days was when they ended. Usually, her mom would be waiting outside her classroom to walk her home, with her little sister asleep in the stroller and her hyperactive Boston Terrier,

Scratch, lunging toward her on the end of his leash. He always acted excited to see her.

Disappointed, but not entirely surprised that her mother didn't show up on this day, Lucy set off toward home on her own. She remembered that today was the day that her mom was supposed to sign the divorce papers.

Jax ran through the crowd of kids toward Lucy. "Hey," he said.

"Hey," she said. "Where were you at lunch today?"

"I had lunch with my dad," Jax said as he pushed his sun streaky blonde hair out of his eyes. "Did you get Mrs. Wheeler for homeroom?"

"Yeah."

"Poor you. I got Mr. Harpt. He seems pretty cool, but everyone says he gives a lot of homework."

Lucy didn't feel like talking much, but was relieved that Jax was there to walk home with her. He lived right next door to the old cottage that Lucy's family inherited two years ago. Since then, they had become close friends, even though he was a boy.

Jax lived with his grandparents because his mom had died and his dad had decided that he couldn't raise a kid on his own. That was all Jax told Lucy that day in his tree house as they watched her dad's moving van drive away. She didn't ask him for any further information.

That was enough to let her know that they had one thing in common—a messed up family.

Sometimes there was just too much to say. They walked home in silence, taking comfort in the other's presence.

Lucy arrived home to the sound of her two-year old sister Mara screaming in the kitchen. She could hear the ear-piercing noise from the yard. Lucy loved her little sister, but hated the bratty and ridiculous fits that she threw almost daily. If Mara was the starring actress of her own drama, Lucy was like the stagehand that was left to clean up after the tantrum. But she cared for her sister, understanding that she was needed to do so. Ever since her mom and dad had split up, Lucy had to take on extra responsibilities.

Hearing the call to duty, Lucy rushed in through the back door to the kitchen, to find her mother, standing right next to her shrieking sister, leaning on the salmon-pink tiled counter with her head in her hands, sobbing. When Lucy appeared, she quickly wiped away her own tears and produced a smile.

"Hi Honey, how was school today?" her mother asked.

Lucy sighed heavily, grabbed a role of paper towels from the counter and began cleaning up the cereal explosion that was created by the little red-faced devil still wailing in her high chair. Cheerios and milk had been chucked across the room and were dripping down the kitchen cabinets and puddling onto the floor, which was already sticky from previous fits and tossing of food. Scratch appeared momentarily to help Lucy's cleaning efforts by licking up any remaining bits of cereal.

Her mother unbuckled the bawling tot from the restraints of her chair, picked her up and hugged her tightly. "It's okay, Love. Shhh," she whispered.

It seemed to Lucy that if one of them wasn't crying, the other one was.

She sopped up the last of the Cheerios and tossed the paper towel into a nearby bucket, which had been left out to catch the water that tended to drip from the ceiling when it rained. "What else could possibly go wrong?" Lucy said under her breath.

"How about if I make you some blackberry cobbler tonight," her mother asked. "To celebrate your first day of middle school?"

"Okay, sure," Lucy said flatly. "I'll take the cobbler, but I'm not sure school is worth celebrating."

"Well then we can celebrate family, okay?" Her mother put her free arm—the one that wasn't holding her baby sister—around Lucy's shoulders and pulled her in for a hug. "Just the girls."

Lucy could see her mother's lip quivering when she pulled away.

"I'll go pick the berries," Lucy said, happy to escape the heavy mood in the kitchen. "Come on Scratch, let's go. See you later!"

Lucy grabbed a metal pail from the back porch and stepped out under the late afternoon sun. As she and Scratch went out the gate and under the shelter of the tall pines that surrounded their home, Lucy's cares drifted away. This, she thought, was just what she needed.

Scratch jogged ahead down the familiar path they had taken so many times before. He sniffed between the moss-covered rocks, stopping near a tree stump to inspect a turquoise colored scarab beetle that had died there. Lucy knelt down to see what he had found.

"Good find, Scratch," she said, inspecting the iridescent bug. "That's one more artifact for our collection. It looks Egyptian. Maybe it's a long lost pet of Cleopatra." She picked it up, and placed the pristine bug gently in the pocket of her sweatshirt.

They sauntered off the footpath, Lucy scanning the forest floor for treasure, Scratch smelling the damp earth and trees. "One day we're going to find something really important," she said.

"Wow! Look at this!" Lucy scooped up a miniature glass bottle she had spied under a fern. "Maybe this was owned by someone very, very small?" She showed this newest item to Scratch and then put it in her pocket with the beetle. "I guess we should get going. We still have to pick berries. Come on, it's this way."

As they moved in the direction of the blackberry bushes, Lucy kicked up dried leaves and crunched them under her feet, listening closely to the subtle noises that she and Scratch made as they walked. But aside from the occasional crack of twigs and footsteps, there was complete stillness. There were no crows cawing or whir of wind gently blowing through the treetops, no squirrels scampering by. Nothing moved except for the walking pair.

For the first time in this familiar landscape, Lucy felt like she was being watched. She put down her pail and slowly slipped on the purple stained gloves that would protect her hands from the prickly thorns as she collected the wild fruit. Goose bumps appeared on her forearms as she looked all around her, hoping not to see what she was feeling. Her whole body tightened as a pinecone fell from above. Scratch growled and barked at the sound.

"Relax, Scratch. It was just a pinecone."

Lucy ignored her dog and her intuition and carried on with the task of gathering berries. But each time she dropped a handful of ripe fruit into her bucket, she looked around for whoever, or whatever, might be out there.

Scratch stood next to Lucy, his big black eyes on alert. The fur on his back bristled.

2

"Ouch!" Lucy yelled, as she yanked her arm away from the thorny blackberry vine that had grabbed her. A long red scrape seeping with blood appeared on the pink underside of her arm where a thorn had raced across the skin. She blotted the graze on her jeans, took off her gardening gloves and picked up the half empty bucket.

Lucy glanced around behind them, still feeling as if she and Scratch were not the only two creatures present in the woods that day. As far as she could see, they were alone, but she couldn't shake the feeling that they weren't. She took a deep breath. "You're just imagining things," she said, reassuring herself aloud.

Besides, if there had been anyone out there, surely Scratch would have continued barking. He was perfectly calm, sitting beneath her. She trusted Scratch to protect her.

"Let's go, Scratch. "I think we've picked enough berries."

Through the still air and long shadows, they briskly followed the tree-lined path for home. Scratch jogged close behind Lucy, stopping to sniff the earth now and again. Lucy nervously snacked on blackberries as she walked, crimson juice dripping down her fingers. As she climbed over a fallen tree, a swarm of black bats flapped wildly toward her from the side of a hill. Startled, she ducked and tried to cover her head, dropping the bucket of blackberries onto the ground.

Scratch started barking ferociously and chased after the bats as they darted between the trees.

"Come back Scratch! It's just a bunch of bats." Lucy laughed at herself for being spooked so easily and bent down to collect the fallen fruit.

"Scratch!" Lucy called as she stood up with the pail in her hand and scanned the now silent greenery for her little black and white friend. She didn't see him anywhere. "Here Boy! Let's go home now!"

But the forest was silent. "Scratch, where are you?" Her voice quivered as she yelled even louder, "Scratch!"

Lucy stepped cautiously down the wooded path, on the alert for sounds from Scratch. Finally, she heard a faint reply. It was a hollow bark that sounded as if it were coming from the bushes just ahead. Following the sound, Lucy discovered a small cave, half hidden behind a cluster of purple flowering vines.

Although Lucy though that she knew every nook and cranny of this forest, she'd never noticed this cave before. "Scratch, are you in there?" she called. One more bark confirmed his presence inside the dark hole.

"Come! Come out, Boy!" She pleaded as she waited at the entrance. She could barely see the white of his fur. But that little lump did not budge. Instead, he whined back at her. That was his usual way of telling her that he wanted something.

"I'm not coming in there. Come out now!"

The cave looked like a giant mouth, ready to eat its visitors.

"Stubborn dog."

Lucy figured that she had to go inside and get Scratch if she wanted to go home any time soon. So she cautiously moved the prickly vines away from the cave entrance, took another deep breath and ducked inside, avoiding the remains of a broken spider web. The sticky strings reached down and clung to her hair and arms.

Once inside, a cool musty quiet surrounded Lucy. As she moved slowly away from the entrance toward Scratch, she was blinded by the darkness of the cave. She felt just like she was in one of those creepy horror films and hoped that there was nothing and no one else in that cave besides the two of them. Lucy squinted, straining to see her little whining dog through the black. She remembered that her new glasses were in her pocket, and although she avoided wearing them unless she had to, this was one of the times that she needed them. Trembling, she put them on and blinked hard to help her eyes adjust to the low light. Within a few seconds, the dimly lit interior came into focus. They were alone in the tiny cave. Scratch was sitting just a few feet away.

The rocky surface of the cave wall was entwined with roots of trees that had grown down from the outside of the small hill that she was now standing under. Cautiously, Lucy moved toward Scratch, avoiding touching anything, and hoping that there were no remaining bats or other critters still in the cave that might be awakened by her presence. But there was evidence that there had been another human in the cave before she and Scratch discovered it, as there was an old oil lantern lying half buried in the dust next to her dog. She bent down and looked more closely, wobbled a little, and steadied herself by leaning against the cool cave wall.

Lucy jerked her hand back as she touched something of a different texture. She slowly felt for it again, and discovered a dirty piece of cloth packed tight into a hole in the cave's wall. She tugged the fabric gently once and then again. Finally Lucy yanked it hard, freeing the fabric from the rocky, root-tangled place that it had been packed into. Along with a cloud of dust, a small wooden box tumbled out of the cloth and down to the cave floor.

"What's this?" She scooped up the box and went toward the light at the front of the cave. Still unable to see it clearly, Lucy rushed out into the daylight. Scratch followed as she ran down the shadowy path to a nearby hillside. They plopped themselves down on the grass to better examine the newly discovered treasure in safety.

The handmade box looked to Lucy like something you might see in an antique shop. Although most of the white paint had been worn away, there were still traces of the crackled color stuck to the wood. On the bottom of the box, someone had carved fancy letters, C.W., and on the top, delicate little roses in the shape of a heart. Tiny rusty hinges creaked when she opened the box lid. Inside the box was a yellowed piece of paper that someone had folded and secreted away.

Lucy plucked the paper gently from the box and read these words:

If you find this talisman, you must keep it a secret.

Tell no one. You have been chosen to be its keeper.

Whoa! This is an amazing find, Lucy thought.

In the box, nestled under the folded paper was a pendant on a lavender velvet cord. She lifted it from its home and dangled the tarnished silver necklace in the light. It was round and heavy and blackened with time. She rubbed it with her t-shirt to reveal a mystical eye that had been crudely engraved in its center. A swirl pattern was primitively drawn around that, and where the eye's iris should have been, was a large amethyst stone that lit up as the sun caught its glittering angles. The backside of the talisman was engraved with the letters *X-I-E-T-U*.

"Freaky," Lucy uttered to the dog at her feet. "This looks like the necklace that my Violet was wearing." She tried to recall exactly the vision she had created earlier in class, but her mind was not providing a repeat performance.

She read the note out loud, again and again, trying to understand its meaning. Lucy wondered if maybe this was one of those "déjà vu" moments that her mom always talked about when something happens that she thought had happened before. But maybe what had happened before was just a clue to what was going to happen later. Maybe Violet had been some sort of premonition that she would find this secret gift.

"I, Lucy, was meant to find this secret talisman. I was chosen. Whatever that means," she said and slipped the velvet cord over her head. She refolded the note, placed it back inside the box and stuffed it in her pocket.

Lucy stood up and grabbed the berry bucket. "Let's go, Scratch," she said as she looked down at the sparkling Xietu talisman around her neck. "This is so cool. It's our own good luck charm. We could use some good luck, huh, Boy?"

As she walked, Lucy analyzed the note and the strange word Xietu. She wondered who had hidden the little box in the cave and how long had it been there. Perhaps it belonged to someone with the initials C.W.? And why did the note insist that she couldn't tell anyone? What would happen if she did? Was the talisman magical? She hoped that it would give her super powers.

Back at home, Lucy snuck past Mara who was dancing with The Wiggles in front of the television while her mother set the dining room table. Lucy dropped off the bucket of berries on the kitchen counter and rushed up the stairs with her secret find.

She took the jewelry cleaner from the bathroom cupboard and disappeared into her room to polish her new treasure. Once she had polished it, the silver shone, and the violet crystal in the center of the eye was so full of light that it almost looked like it was glowing.

The talisman sparkled on Lucy's neck, as she looked at her reflection in the dresser mirror. She felt special and almost pretty with it on. Lucy wanted to wear it, hidden under her t-shirt, but decided that would be too risky. She couldn't take any chances that her mother might notice something different about her. And the note said that she had to keep it a secret. She feared that if she didn't, the luck she hoped it was going to bring her might not be good.

It was killing her that she couldn't run next door and show her friend Jax what she had found. The Xietu talisman would make him jealous for sure! He was also an expert finder of treasure in the woods. Jax had even purchased a metal detector with his allowance, for the sole purpose of "finding something worth a lot of money" so he could buy more video games. Together, so far, they had found wire-rimmed eyeglasses, a few buffalo nickels, a pair of silver dice, and some other junk.

Jax kept the coins in a gallon jar in his tree house, and Lucy kept the rest. For Lucy, the value of these items was in their stories, and she spent many late nights creating wild characters and elaborate plots that gave importance to these objects that had been lost or forgotten.

The day that had started off badly had gotten better, and the night had ended splendidly, all because of her new good luck charm. Her mother and Mara managed to get through dinner without any meltdowns, and the blackberry cobbler with vanilla ice cream was delicious. Lucy smiled as she cleared the table and did the dishes after dinner, all the while thinking about the secret talisman that had already begun to change her world for the better.

She hugged her mother and went upstairs to her room, slipped the jeweled pendant over her neck and began imagining herself as queen of the forest and keeper of the talisman. After all, she had been *chosen* to be just that.

That night, Lucy fell asleep with her pen in her hand and the journal that she wrote all her stories in still open on her bed. Scratch was next to her. Each night after her mom would go to sleep, Scratch would sneak upstairs to Lucy's room and burrow his little body under the covers next to her.

But her sweet slumber ended abruptly when she heard a distant cry. Lucy cracked opened her eyes and pulled the covers up over her nose. What was that?

It was normal for her rustic home to creak and groan at night. Her mother always excused the creepy noises as "old house sounds" and told Lucy she shouldn't worry about them.

She held her breath, hoping that she wouldn't hear the high-pitched moan again, and watched as the moonlight cast twisted shadows on the wall through her bedroom window. The wind scratched dried leaves along the roof.

There it went again. No, it wasn't the tree outside or the house complaining of old age. It was definitely a whimper, Lucy thought, as if someone or something was hurt. The whiny voice soon became louder and began to sound famil-iar. Lucy moved her leg under the covers, feeling that Scratch was no longer in his usual spot.

Scratch's calls were coming from downstairs. Lucy knew that something was wrong.

3

Lucy ran down the steps, skipping the fourth one from the top to avoid the creaky sound that would inevitably wake her mother, who had creaky step and baby crying radar. For every other sound, she did not wake—obviously. Downstairs, Lucy saw lights flashing in the darkened living room. She peeked around the corner to find her mother sleeping soundly under a blanket on the sofa, the TV still on and a glass of wine half empty on the coffee table.

Lucy found Scratch lying on his belly; all four legs sprawled out on the cool floor of the laundry room, seemingly unable to move. "Scratch, what's wrong? Are you okay?" she asked, kneeling beside him.

She held her breath and tried not to gag as she cleaned up the barf, red and rancid and lumpy with blackberries.

Then she sat down on the floor next to her ailing dog, who had obviously eaten too many dropped berries this afternoon. This had happened before, when he had eaten some unknown nuts on one of their expeditions through the forest. He eventually had thrown them up and was immediately better afterward. Lucy waited for Scratch to perk up, but this time, he was not getting up off the floor.

As she stared into the big round eyes of her closest ally in life, the tears began to race down Lucy's face. She absolutely could not bear the thought of anything bad happening to Scratch.

After about an hour of petting, Lucy remembered that she was still wearing the good luck talisman that they had found in the woods that day. She lifted it from her t-shirt, held it between her hands, and wished for Scratch to be well again. Soon, they both drifted off to sleep, Lucy propped up against the warm metal of the dryer and Scratch's head resting in her lap. She woke to his wet tongue bathing the back of her hand.

"Are you feeling better?" she whispered, and scooped up the little dog to take him up to her room to sleep the rest of the night under her watch.

* * *

The next morning, Lucy woke to the sun streaming in her bedroom window and Scratch lying next to her under the covers, snoring. He was obviously okay, but instead of his usual morning antics of jumping on Lucy and licking her face the minute she opened her eyes, Scratch just lay there and rolled over on his back to cue her to rub his pink belly, which she did.

"I have to get you back downstairs to your own bed before Mom sees you," she said and picked up the lethargic dog in her arms. Lucy draped a few pieces of dirty clothes over Scratch so that she could sneak him past her mother, who she could hear was already awake and tending to Mara in the kitchen. While she strapped Mara into her high chair, Lucy and Scratch slipped past unnoticed and quietly closed the laundry room door.

Lucy put Scratch down on his pillow and proceeded to serve him his morning kibble, but when he refused food, Lucy knew it was serious. She pushed open the door and called for help. "Mom, Scratch is sick! Look. He won't even eat," Lucy said. Her voice was strained with emotion.

Lucy's mom looked towards the laundry room and answered, "He looks fine to me. What are you so upset about?" She handed Mara her sippy-cup from the fridge.

"Well, he's not fine! Last night I heard him crying, so I came down to see what was wrong. He had thrown up everywhere, and I had to clean it up! I can't believe you didn't hear him! You were asleep right there on the sofa."

"Please stop shouting Lucy! I have a headache." She rubbed her forehead and walked toward her daughter. She bent down to pet the dog. "I'm sorry, Scratch. What's wrong with you Boy?"

Scratch barely moved as she stroked his fur.

"Lucy, I understand that you are upset, but I don't see anything wrong with him. Would you feel better if we took him to the vet this afternoon?"

"Yes. Can I stay home from school, and we'll go now? I don't want to leave him."

"You have to go to school. Don't worry, I'll look after him," her mother assured her. "I'll make an appointment for later today. I promise. Now go get ready for school"

Lucy stomped back upstairs to her room. After getting dressed, she slipped her new lucky charm in her sweatshirt pocket. "This thing better work," she said to herself.

* * *

After school, her mom was waiting in the car with the napping baby and Scratch, who was lying on a towel on the floor in the back seat.

"How is he?" Lucy asked, reaching between the seats to pet him.

"He's fine, Honey," her mother said. Lucy noticed that she smiled at her in the same fake way that she always did when she was trying to hide something. "How was school today?"

"Fine," Lucy said. "Did he throw up again?"

"No, he's been sleeping peacefully all day." Her mom hummed along to a song on the radio—another clue that she was lying.

Lucy didn't take her eyes off Scratch the entire way to the vet's office. She felt her jeans for the Xietu, which was heavy in her pocket.

Once they arrived, her mom took Scratch into the examining room while Lucy babysat Mara in the reception area.

"No Mara!" Lucy said.

Mara had just reached her hand into a jar of doggie treats that were available for their four-legged customers. When she bent down to pick up her little sister and save her from eating the beef flavored treats, the shiny talisman fell out of her pocket and landed with a thud on the floor. Mara squealed with delight, scampered toward the fallen pendant, grabbed it, and shoved it directly into her mouth. Before Lucy could snatch it back, it was covered in slimy saliva.

"Give me that," Lucy whispered as she pried it from her sister's juicy fingers and quickly slid the wet talisman back into her jeans pocket.

"Mine!" Mara yelled, followed by some other nonsensical sounds.

"Shhhh! Look at this Mara!" Lucy lifted her sister into her lap and attempted to distract her with a picture book, all the while, worrying about Scratch and that someone besides her baby sister may have seen the talisman. Mara couldn't tell anyone about the Xietu; so technically, Lucy's secret was still safe unless somebody else had noticed.

Her mother, who had taken Scratch into the examining room, came out about thirty minutes later holding their limp dog in her arms.

"Lucy jumped up and ran to him. "No! What's wrong?" She tried to hold back the tears as she felt his body for signs of life.

"He's okay. He's just sleeping," her mom said.

"I'll call with the test results," said the veterinary's assistant who helped her mother out the door and gave her a plastic prescription bottle full of pills for Scratch.

"Mom, is he going to be okay?" Lucy asked as she swallowed the emotion in her throat.

"I'll explain in the car. Let's go."

"Come on Mara," Lucy said, taking Mara's hand.

Her mother gently laid Scratch in the back seat of the car and turned to answer her daughter with an unconvincing smile. "The vet said that he is very sick, but that the medicine will help him feel better. Don't worry, Lucy, he's going to be fine."

Lucy didn't believe her. She could tell when her mother was not telling the whole truth because she tended to bite her lip when she was uncomfortable—and she was doing just that, Lucy noticed, as she drove them home.

During the long ride, Lucy worried in silence. She wondered if the Xietu could cure Scratch. She thought it made him better last night, but obviously it hadn't. In fact, he was perfectly healthy until she found that secret talisman in the cave. Maybe his illness was caused by it, and instead of bringing her good luck; it had intensified her bad luck.

Leave it to me to be 'chosen' to find something that would make me even unluckier, she thought. I can't let Scratch pay the price.

By the time they reached home, Lucy had convinced herself that she must put the ill-fated treasure back in the cave from which it came. After making Scratch comfortable on his bed in the laundry room, she went to her room and collected the wooden box with the note inside, and the threadbare fabric that the treasure had been wrapped in. While her mom was fixing dinner, she grabbed a flashlight from the laundry room cupboard and slipped away, down the wooded path to find the cave and return the Xietu talisman to its former home.

When she approached, the sound of her footsteps roused a pack of dark winged shadows that burst from the dark hole into the dusky sky. Lucy shone her light into the cave and crept inside to find the place where this unlucky bundle had once been hidden. She frantically stuffed it back inside the hole in the wall for someone else to discover, and for someone else to have its bad luck.

Lucy raced home and threw open the door to the laundry home. She sat down on the floor next to Scratch and loved him until her mom called her for dinner. She wanted to make him feel better, just as he always did for her when her world was coming to an end as she knew it.

"I'm sorry Scratch, she said. I wish I had never found that bad luck Xietu in the first place."

4

The moon seemed extra big and bright that night as Lucy watched for shooting stars out her second story bedroom window. Scratch's soft fur was warm against her side, and his little smooshed in nose was peeking out of the covers as he slept. Lucy didn't want to sleep. She told herself that she shouldn't sleep until she saw a star fall. She needed to counteract the bad luck of the talisman and make a wish for Scratch to get better. Whatever her mother said, Lucy knew deep down, that her dog was terribly sick. If he weren't, her mom would not have allowed her to bring Scratch up to her room for the night.

The starry sky was still, and Lucy's heavy eyelids kept closing. She took off her glasses, rubbed her eyes and got

out of bed to sneak downstairs for a snack, avoiding the noisy step, so as not to get caught. The chocolate chip cookies that her mom had baked that evening were still sitting out on the counter, so she grabbed two, a glass of milk, and a dog biscuit for Scratch. If there was one thing that Lucy could count on her mother doing, it was baking her cares away. She scrambled back up to her room with the treats.

"Scratch, I brought you something," Lucy whispered and pulled back the bed covers to see if Scratch wanted the biscuit she had brought for him. But Scratch wasn't there! Where could he have gone? He must have needed to go out, and he'll come right back, she thought. She sat down at her desk by the window to wait for him and watch for stars while she ate the cookies.

It seemed to Lucy that Scratch had been gone for long enough. She checked the digital alarm clock; She remembered that she had gotten up at 11:11. It was 11:30. It was time to go look for him. Lucy looked out the window and down to the dewy lawn below. As if he was waiting to be found, Scratch sat on the cold ground below, looking up to Lucy's window, as if he were waiting for her to notice him. When she did, he began barking like crazy.

Geez! What is that dog doing? She unlocked the brass window latch and pushed the wooden frames opened. The cool night air rushed in.

"Shhh! Scratch, be quiet or Mom will hear you!"

Scratch stopped barking for a second and then continued even louder than before.

"Come on, Boy, come inside!" But Scratch just sat there in the grass, staring up at Lucy, his wide mouth smiling. "Scratch, you shouldn't be out there in the cold. Look I brought you a treat. Come get it!" she said, holding up the bone-shaped biscuit.

But Scratch could not be bribed inside and stayed exactly where he was. Lucy grabbed the patchwork quilt from the foot of her bed, wrapped it around her shoulders and carefully tiptoed down the stairs again. Her rubber rain boots were waiting at the door, and she stepped into them as she grabbed Scratch's leash off the coat hooks. She turned the doorknob and headed outside to try and coax the stubborn little creature into the house.

"Scratch, don't you want to come inside?" she asked, as she squatted down on the wooden planks of the front porch with the treat in her outstretched hand.

He didn't budge. He just stood there with his big, cute eyes, whining at her to come towards him. With each step that Lucy took towards Scratch, he inched back. Just as she got within grabbing range, the chubby little pooch took off running across the yard, towards the tall cedar fence. The fence kept him from going into the woods that bordered their house. Scratch had run off before and gotten lost in the forest, so Lucy's dad had to put up a fence to keep him safe. Scratch ran to the gate, sat himself down and continued barking.

Now, Lucy was beginning to get irritated by this behavior. It was freezing cold and she wanted to be back in her own bed. "Uurgh! Scratch! Come on, please. Come inside, Boy!" Again, her calling did not help. She didn't have much choice but to follow him out under the moonlit sky.

So she stepped off the front porch and onto the pebbled path that led to the front gate. Scratch was wagging his stubby little tail and jumping up and down with excitement.

She pulled her quilt tighter around her shoulders and dragged her feet down the walk in her heavy boots, noticing that she could see her breath mist in the cold for the first time this fall. "Come on! Let's go inside where it's warm. Please!" She bent down to try and catch hold of his collar at the gate, but Scratch dodged her grasp again.

As Lucy stood up, she caught sight of a small cluster of twinkling lights, floating around in the lower branches of the pine trees just beyond their property. Could be fireflies, she thought, but it seems a little bright for bugs. Whatever it was, the starry mass was far beyond her range of sight without her glasses.

Scratch began pawing at the gate. "Is that what you wanted to show me?" she asked the skittish pup.

Lucy wasn't sure if she had lost her mind to even be considering going out into the forest alone at night. Whatever the case, she was mesmerized by the mysterious light show and something compelled her to open the gate. She flipped the latch. Scratch squeezed himself out of the partly opened door and took off running towards the glow in the trees.

Aside from the moonlight on the treetops, it was very dark out there under the canopy of pines, and Lucy was even more scared than she had been when she wandered into that unknown cave. Her mom would kill her if she knew that she was outside alone at this late hour. But now that she had freed Scratch from the confines of their property, she had no choice. She had to follow and make sure that he was okay.

Scratch ran ahead, the white of his fur being the only part of him that Lucy could still see as he navigated the trees. He barked at her to follow. She ran behind, her heart racing, and her rubber boots thumping over the damp ground. It appeared as if the glow that Scratch was chasing was moving too, guiding them deeper and deeper into the forest. They had already passed the cave where the Xietu was, and were coming closer to the lake. Lucy felt like she would never catch up to Scratch, until finally the sphere of lights hovered in a small clearing, and Scratch sat down, right under the brightly sparkling vision that they had seen from afar.

Lucy slowed down as she approached the unknown cautiously, but Scratch was not afraid, calmly basking in the pale violet glow that it cast on him. His wide mouth turned up and his pink tongue hung out of his silly smile. He looked thoroughly pleased to be showing Lucy his discovery!

As she crept closer, the strange orb of sparks became clearer. It appeared to be several balls of light that were moving so fast that they created a light trail, and together, a larger shimmering circle of light. Lucy gasped as it flew straight toward her. Her body seemed to freeze in time. Right before her eyes, the unified light began to separate into individual sparkling shapes that looked something like birds or possibly even extremely large bugs. But their light was so bright and their movement so erratic, that Lucy could not tell what they were!

"Whoa, this can't be happening," Lucy murmured, as the bird/bug shapes slowed to a humming blur of pale colors with arms and legs—and glistening lavender wings! They looked sort of like tiny glimmering girl birds, or large female butterflies, or they could be some type of fairy-creature, Lucy decided. But it was dark and she hadn't worn her glasses, so she couldn't see them very clearly.

Lucy squinted at the vision before her. Is this real? She remembered the other girl-creature that she named Violet.

Violet was regular girl size, at least she though she was when she saw her outside her classroom window, and she turned out not to be real at all. Lucy wondered if this mini gang of sparkling girls was another figment of her imagination?

So in order to confirm that she was not dreaming up these tiny flying creatures, she decided to see if she could touch one and feel that it was real. She lifted up her hand and grabbed into space wildly, taking hold of one's leg, but the spry little thing wriggled away.

"Hey, watch it! Give me back my boot!" the winged girl called out angrily to Lucy as she flew out of reach.

Lucy looked down to find a teeny-tiny leather boot in her hand. I'm definitely not imagining them, she thought.

These girl-creatures created a blur of light around Lucy's head as they circled her like little hummingbirds around a flower. She was getting dizzy from spinning in circles, trying to see them.

"Stop! What are you?" she yelled. "Are you fairies?"

They stopped immediately and hovered in the air, now right in front of her.

"No, stupid," one voice said, clearly annoyed by Lucy's ignorance. "We are VamPixies!"

"VamPixies? I don't understand," Lucy said cautiously, wondering why they looked so frighteningly real and not cartoonish. "What is a VamPixie, anyway?"

A tiny white-haired girl moved closer to Lucy, and in a soft-spoken voice, said, "We are actually an ancient tribe of ...um. . ."

She stopped and looked back at her friends for approval and then continued. "Let's just say, well, we are a blend."

"A blend of what?" Lucy asked the beautiful, yet ghostly looking creature.

The girl smiled and answered slowly, "Vam-Pixie. Get it?"

Lucy stared back at her blankly. Her brain felt foggy. Maybe the fairy girls had done something to her?

The girl whispered softly, "Vampire-Pixie," but don't be afraid.

5

ONCE the little pixies—the VamPixies—had made their status clear, Lucy studied the creatures before her. She noticed that their wings were different from what she would expect a fairy to have. They were pointy and shaped like a bat's wing. And their miniature clothes were made of rich fabrics, trimmed in ribbons and lace—also not very fairy-like. Fairies would probably wear dresses made out of leaves and flowers, and they would have slippers with curled-up toes, Lucy thought. These girls wore fine leather boots with buckles and buttons, like the tiny one she still held.

Lucy examined the milky skinned, white-haired girl that hovered near. The girl returned an uncomfortable smile, exposing her fangless teeth between her red-stained lips, and then tucked her hair behind her pointed ears. Lucy thought

that she looked to be near her own age, maybe a little older, but she couldn't be certain. This VamPixie's clothes were a wash of lace and pale tones, and her skin was so light that aside from her tiny red mouth, she looked almost colorless.

"What's your name?" Lucy asked.

The tiny girl smiled, "Snow."

Well, Lucy thought, that fits—exactly.

Still feeling a little dazed, Lucy stood silently as the other VamPixies, who had been dangling in the air behind Snow until now, came forward and introduced themselves.

The next girl buzzed up to Lucy's nose, and announced herself as, "Scarlet." Her introduction was decidedly brief. Right after she said her name, she tossed her red hair, turned on the heels of her matching red boots and flew back in line with the others, as if she had said everything she needed to say. Scarlet folded her arms over her chest and peered back at Lucy from under her crimson bangs.

"Hello, my name is Aluna," said the girl who was missing a boot. The corners of her mouth turned up politely at Lucy as she pointed to her left stocking foot. "May I please have my boot back?"

Lucy held the miniature granny style boot up in her open palm.

Aluna dove forward, snatched it up, and attempted to untie the laces of her boot with one hand. When she nearly dropped it, she scowled and flew up to a low-hanging branch above her. She sat down, loosened the laces, and slipped it back over her lacey leg. Aluna quickly returned with her boot back on, and righted herself by tugging down on the bottom of the vintage corset that cinched in her waist. Then she smoothed her hands over her skirt and pushed her caramel colored curls off her face. "Pleased to meet you," Aluna said.

One last small girl with blonde wavy hair peeked out shyly from behind the others and waved at Lucy. "I'm Opal," she said, and giggled nervously. Her tiny hands looked like they were stained with red paint, or maybe it was something else, Lucy wasn't sure. But as she inspected Opal's soiled clothes, she could see that there were green and blue drips of paint down her top and onto the frothy layers of fabric that made up her skirt. Her hair was a bit disheveled, like she had just rolled out of bed.

Lucy's feet felt as if they had become a part of the earth she stood on, rooted into the forest floor and unable to move. Her mind felt tingly, and she heard each word the VamPixies spoke echo through her brain. But there was one word that finally broke the spell of entrancement she was under.

"Wait a minute! Did you just say VAMPIRES?" Lucy backed up slowly, just in case they might try to bite her.

The VamPixies smiled apologetically.

"Ooohhhhkkaaayyy! I think we need to go! Come on Scratch!"

She was just about to run right back to the safety of her own bed when Snow shouted, "Wait, don't go! We have come to heal your dog!"

The other three creatures quickly called out, one by one, "Oh, don't be scared! We won't hurt you! Please stay! We never harm anyone! We have a code that we live by and have vowed never to break the VamPixie Promise."

And then the four tiny girls in lavender bat wings joined hands, hanging in the air before Lucy's wide eyes, and recited their promise:

Friends forever, we stick together,

As sisters of the night.

With pure hearts and healing hands,

There will be no bloody bite.

Peaceful guardians of Xiemoon,

We promise to do right.

And listen to the wise Moon,

She is our guiding light.

VamPixies Forever!

Lucy searched their lovely faces and considered what they promised—friendship, healing, no blood, to be peaceful guards of somewhere or other, and listening to the moon. Those were all good things—she guessed. And by appearances, the

VamPixies seemed nice enough. She didn't see any fangs when they smiled at her. Besides she was substantially larger than the lot of them put together. If they did try to bite her, she could probably squash them easily enough. Most importantly, there was the part about saving Scratch. If they could help him, she needed to stick around and find out how.

She gazed up at the moon above the four luminous creatures before her, wiggled her toes in her boots and took a deep breath, hoping that her decision not to run was the right one. She wasn't quite sure what to do next, so she introduced herself. "Um, my name is Lucy, and this is Scratch."

"Hello!" They all said together.

"How did you know that Scratch was sick?" Lucy asked.

"The moon told us that you needed our help, so we came right away," Snow explained with a kind smile. "Then once we arrived and felt Scratch's energy, which was very low, we knew immediately that we had been called here to save him. We are healers."

"Huh?" Lucy uttered. "The moon speaks to you?"

"Well, kind of," Opal said, twisting her blonde locks around her finger. "It's more like she gives us signals or astral insights."

Lucy was even more confused by Opal's cryptic explanation. "Okay, well, no offense, but how can a bunch of little pixie girls heal my dog?"

Scarlet shook her fiery head and let out what sounded like a growl at Lucy. She was obviously very offended by Lucy's remark. She darted forward, stopped just short of Lucy's nose and said, "We certainly could do a better job than a falling star!"

The others snickered, but Snow grabbed Scarlet's wing from behind and pulled her back away from Lucy. "We may be small," Snow said, "but our magic is very strong. We have the power to heal your dog, but there is one small issue that you need to consider. If we save his life, there will be a cost. Scratch will become a true creature of the night, sprouting wings like ours every night at dusk."

Aluna fluttered nearer to Lucy and said. "He will also become immortal. Like us, he will live on forever and never die."

"Will he become miniature too?" Lucy asked with concern.

"Oh no! Scratch will stay exactly the same, except for the wings of course, which will only grow at night. As long as you hide him away at dusk, nobody will know he is a VamPixie, except for you." Aluna assured her.

"So, Scratch will grow glittery wings," Lucy clarified out loud. "And he won't be sick anymore, and he won't die, not ever?" As she asked the question, she remembered the horrible day that she had spent at the vet with her mother. Even though her mom wouldn't admit that Scratch was dying, Lucy had a bad feeling—really bad, that her mother was lying.

Snow answered, "Yes, he will live. But only you can know his secret. If we heal him, you cannot tell anyone. After tonight, we do not exist. No one can know about us!"

"I promise that I won't let anyone find out about you, or your healing powers. You can trust me," she assured them, agreeing because she knew that this was her dog's only chance to live.

But Lucy's enthusiasm dwindled when she remembered the unappealing vampire quality that might present a problem for her later. She asked, "But will I have to feed him blood?"

Scarlet threw up her arms and said, "I am so tired of being stereotyped! VamPixies are not vampires—I mean, we are, but we aren't. As we told you before, we are a violence free society, and WE DO NOT SUCK BLOOD!" With this last declaration, Scarlet turned away from Lucy and huffed off, passing under a tree branch and accidentally knocking the miniature top hat that she had been wearing off of her head. She made that growling sound again and darted down to retrieve her fallen hat.

Aluna explained, "No, Scratch will only need a few sweet snacks for energy each day. VamPixies feed on sugar, not on blood! Sugar tastes so much better, and it satisfies our hunger. I can't understand why anyone would want to drink blood anyway. I mean…cupcakes or blood?" she asked Lucy, demonstrating her choice by using her hands as unbalanced scales in the favor of cupcakes.

"Well, I've never tasted blood. How do you know?" Lucy asked.

Snow nudged Aluna, as if to tell her to be quiet. "Well, she doesn't actually know because any VamPixie who is caught drinking blood would be banished from our society. We simply do not allow it. Aluna was just presuming."

Lucy looked down at Scratch who was listening attentively at her feet. As his watery dark eyes stared up at her, her heart felt like it was being wrung out like a dishrag in her chest. She believed deep down, that her only choice was to trust the VamPixies to heal Scratch, vampires or not. If she refused their help, he would die. She could not face losing him, and this was the only chance she had to save her best friend.

Lucy took a deep breath before she spoke. "Please heal my dog."

The VamPixies, including Scarlet who had recovered from her fit, flew low and hovered in a circle around Scratch. They lifted their right hands and made what looked to Lucy like a peace sign with their fingers. Lucy guessed that the peace sign also stood for VamPixie because it made a V-shape.

One by one, the girls pointed their Secret Sign at Scratch and repeated their promise once again.

Friends forever, we stick together,

As sisters of the night.

With pure hearts and healing hands,

There will be no bloody bite.

Peaceful guardians of Xiemoon,

We promise to do right.

And listen to the wise Moon,

She is our guiding light.

VamPixies Forever!

With the last words of their promise, the VamPixies' fingers began to glow with a vibrant pink light. And then, the healing happened—no magic wand, just two electric fingers that slowly sent a beam of light through the darkness and created an aura of energy around her little dog. Lucy worried that they were hurting him at first, but Scratch remained calm and peaceful as radiant light enveloped him. She held her breath, with her eyes fixed on Scratch, as a cluster of dark purple lights bubbled up out of his back and floated within this healing aura of energy. Finally, the violet sparks fizzled out like burned up fireworks, dropping to the ground beside Scratch as hard black stones.

As the rose-colored haze and residual smoke from the VamPixie's electrical display of magic began to fade, Scratch's pudgy form reappeared. Lucy noticed that his coat looked shiny and sleek in the moonlight. She waited for a sign that their powers had actually healed him, without turning him into some kind of rabid VamPixie freak. When Scratch's long pink tong dropped from his smiling mouth, Lucy's worries faded away. He stood up, shook his body, and barked at her.

"Scratch, you're okay!" Lucy said.

She bent down to pet him, but before her hand reached his back, Scratch began to whimper. Lucy gasped and turned toward the tiny healers.

"What did you do to him?"

"I never should have trusted anyone who is part vampire," Lucy said. Her face was flushed with anger, and she swiped the air to catch the VamPixies. "You lied to me! You hurt my dog, and now I'm going to hurt you!"

The VamPixies scattered, flying out of reach. Snow, who narrowly escaped Lucy's grasp, yelled back at her, "We didn't hurt him!"

Lucy felt her throat close and her eyes well up with tears when she heard the cries of her dog. She looked at Scratch, helpless and unable to stop the pain he was in. The fur on his back began to bubble, followed by two small points that tented his flesh and quickly poked through his fur. The glistening lavender skins spread out like a new chick's wings. Scratch had become a full-fledged VamPixie.

The VamPixies buzzed around Scratch, pointing their tiny healing fingers at the wounded skin where his wings had erupted. His whimpering stopped instantly.

Scratch, who looked surprised to see that his body had these new appendages, began to jump and flap his glittering wings awkwardly. Lucy laughed at her excited puppy, who took a running leap and lifted off the ground, wings beating the air, nearly getting caught in the low branches of the pine trees, and finally soaring above the treetops. Lucy beamed as she watched Scratch fly high above and eventually back down to the mossy ground where she waited with the VamPixies.

"I'm sorry," Lucy said to the VamPixies. "Thank you for helping us. I promise I won't tell anyone about his wings or how he got them."

"You're welcome," Snow said with a smile. "I suppose we should be going now."

As Lucy watched Scratch flap his glittery wings, she thought how good it must feel to be able to fly. She considered her own life and how she might like to just fly away from it all. She was tired of cleaning up after her sister and doing chores. Even her mother, who had always been there for her, was too busy crying about her own problems to care about Lucy's. Yes, she thought, I want to fly.

"Wait!" Lucy called after the VamPixies. "I want a pair of those wings. I would like to be a VamPixie too."

The tiny girls stopped their exit and laughed hysterically at Lucy.

"You can't do that!" Scarlet said. "You don't need to become a VamPixie. You are a healthy girl. Besides, don't you have a family and friends that would wonder what happened to you if you suddenly disappeared after dark? Where will you hide?"

Lucy shrugged her shoulders in response.

Snow said, "If you become a VamPixie, you will not be able to be a normal girl anymore!"

"Yeah, I know! That's okay with me. In fact, I think that would be kind of awesome," Lucy said. All she could think about was being able to fly around with Scratch after dark and have a secret identity. To her, it sounded like the perfect escape from her dreadful life. "I promise I will keep my wings a secret. Please, please, please!" she pleaded with them.

"You see, Lucy, Scratch would have died if we did not heal him. He NEEDED to become a VamPixie," Aluna said. "It was a matter of life or death."

"And you don't NEED to become one of us," Snow added.

"Well, then how can I become a VamPixie?" Lucy persisted.

All four VamPixies looked at each other and agreed. "You can't," they said.

"We don't allow mortal girls into our secret world, or grant them VamPixie status just because they want a pair of glittery wings," Scarlet said as she fluttered her own in the moonlight.

Opal nervously stated her view to Lucy and the other VamPixies. "Perhaps there is one way that you could become a VamPixie...I mean, an Honorary Member of the Secret Society of VamPixies, that is.

The others looked at Opal and shook their heads. "I really don't think we should do this. I doubt that Salu would approve," Snow added.

"Oh come on! I want to go to your world!" Lucy said, but her begging didn't appear to sway the opinions of Aluna, Scarlet, or Snow.

Lucy's only hope was Opal, who appeared to be on her side because Lucy heard her say, "We could teach her everything," as she huddled closely with the others. "But why can't we teach a girl from The Outside our secrets?" Opal asked her VamPixie sisters.

Scarlet scoffed at Opal's suggestion. "Because she's mortal. Duh!"

Lucy pretended that she wasn't paying attention while the VamPixies argued amongst themselves, but she was trying her hardest to hear them discussing her fate.

While she waited, she looked around at the sky full of stars, the big moon, and the forest of trees around her. Lucy hoped that the VamPixies would give her a chance. If they accepted her, she might get to be the exciting girl that she longed to be, with jeweled wings, magical powers, and cool new friends. Jax was great and all, but he couldn't fly or cast magic spells, and he certainly didn't understand girl stuff. Yes, she would miss her mom and Mara, but with all that was going on at home, it would be nice to escape to a new life, at least for a while.

"If I snuck out at night, nobody would even notice I was gone," she mumbled to herself.

Opal finally broke away from their circle, flew toward Lucy and removed a tiny charm that hung around her neck. "Here, take this key!"

Lucy held out her hand to catch the miniscule key. Opal dropped it into her palm, where it instantly grew to fit her hand! Lucy stared in wonder at this magical item. It was not like the modern keys she used, but an old-fashioned skeleton type, tied with a lavender ribbon. It was made of tarnished gold, the head shaped like a rose with jewels set along the curves of its petals, and the key end shaped like bat wings.

"This key can open the door to our world," Opal said. "If Salu approves, we will come for you under the next moon."

Lucy slid the velvet ribbon over her head and felt the weight of the secret key, hanging heavy around her neck. "Who's Salu?" Lucy asked.

"Salu is our VamPixie elder and our teacher," Opal answered. "She is the High Priestess and Peacekeeper of our land."

As Lucy clutched the key and thought about the potential freedom that it represented, the glowing otherworldly girls began to transform back into a whir of sparkling light and quickly disappeared into the darkness from which they had come.

Alone in the forest again, Lucy was grateful to have the soft glow of Scratch's wings to guide them home. Clutching the blanket around her shoulders and jogging behind her flying dog, she imagined herself wearing a pair of those jeweled wings and soaring next to Scratch in their VamPixie life of luxury. But Lucy's sparkling thoughts were quickly interrupted.

From behind her, a pack of shadowy wings darted in and around her head. Lucy screamed, ducked and waved her arms wildly to frighten them away, nearly dropping the quilt. She looked left and right, checking for other life that might exist in the darkness and sprinted to catch up to Scratch with his glowing appendages. Unlike the VamPixies, the bats that swarmed her did not feel so friendly.

Lucy could see the wooden gate to her house ahead. Her heart pounded in her chest as she threw open the door to safety.

* * *

The next day passed slowly for Lucy. She counted the minutes for each class to end and the school day to finish, trying not to smile openly when she thought about the secret adventure that awaited her. She couldn't wait to get home, practice guitar, help with dinner and dishes, and do her homework so that darkness and bedtime would arrive.

After faking her nightly routine and saying goodnight to her mom, Lucy closed her bedroom door and changed from her pajamas into jeans and a sweater so that she would be ready to go when the VamPixies arrived.

Earlier that evening, before it got dark, Lucy had hidden Scratch in the old barn out back. She couldn't chance having her mom find out about his wings, so she made Scratch a cozy bed in the old horse stalls and asked him to stay there until the VamPixies came. There was enough room in the barn for Scratch to fly around with his new wings, and she was certain that no one would find him there.

For the next two hours, Lucy heard every tick of the alarm clock next to her bed. She began to worry that her miniature friends weren't coming. Opal did explain they would only come for her if the High Priestess approved of their plan to make her an Honorary Member of their secret VamPixie club. Maybe she said no, Lucy considered.

"I am so tired of waiting." Lucy said, as she lay stretched out on her bed, fiddling with the skeleton key that could open their secret world. "I wish I knew where the door was."

Lucy finally succumbed to the boredom and disappointment she felt. While staring blankly at the moon outside, she dozed off, only to be awakened by the sound of Scratch whining and yapping right outside her second story window. Lucy opened her eyes to see him hovering in the air, flapping wildly to maintain his position until she noticed him.

"Scratch, keep it down! Someone will hear you!" Lucy said, as she motioned for Scratch to be quiet through the closed window. She grabbed her jacket, snuck down the stairs and ran for the door.

As soon as Lucy was outside, Scratch, who had grounded himself to wait for her, took off running. His chubby little body lifted as his sparkly wings beat the air. She ran after his moon-glowing appendages that illuminated the way for the two of them to see through the dark forest.

Lucy looked to the trail behind her as she climbed over fallen trees and hopped over rocks. She thought she could hear footsteps other than her own, just like she did when they were picking berries. She slowed a bit and looked around through the darkness, but she couldn't see anything outside of the glow that Scratch was providing. Lucy ran faster to catch up with Scratch. He was leading her deeper into the forest, toward the lake—the one where her family used to have picnics in the summer.

Lucy followed Scratch's sparkling wings to the footbridge over the ravine, and stopped. She saw something new on the opposite bank of the river. Just ahead was what looked to be, a never-ending wall of vines that did not exist the last time she and Scratch had walked this trail. The winding vines climbed all the way up into the pale blue mist. This barrier spanned the forest, left and right, obviously to keep trespassers in or out, Lucy wasn't sure which. But right in the center of the wall of green was an archway covered with beautiful red roses and white stars of light.

The twinkling lights that adorned the rose vine reminded Lucy of the parties that her family used to have in their garden. Her mom loved to decorate by stringing tiny white lights throughout their garden and around the trees, turning their yard into a magical fairyland.

Lucy squeezed her eyes closed to make certain that when she opened them again, the wall of vines and the twinkling rose covered arch was in fact, really there. It was, and under the trellis was a swirl of glittering light, inviting Lucy and Scratch to pass through. It was the VamPixies! Scratch had led her to the secret door to meet them.

Lucy continued over the creaky planks of the wooden bridge to the opening in the divide between her world and the unknown.

"Look Scratch, they're here!" Lucy said, as she bent down to pet her wiggling friend, who had landed in the grass next to her. "They've come for us."

Lucy smiled, took a deep breath, and started to walk under the arch of flowers. But as she stepped forward, her toe kicked something solid and then her forehead knocked against what seemed to be a boundary between her world and theirs. "Ouch!" she yelled, reaching out to feel the clear glassy surface that stopped her. Scratch began barking wildly, as Lucy slid her hand across the cold barrier. Even the glow of VamPixie wings that she recognized on the other side of the door had disappeared.

Lucy wasn't sure what to do next, as she stood blankly before the promise of a magical new life that she couldn't reach. She saw the invisible door begin to fog up, as if someone's breathe on the cold surface had caused it to mist. And then, in backwards letters, someone, or something wrote in the foggy surface: yeK ruoY esU. Lucy stepped back, quickly pulled out her glasses from her pocket and read the jumbled words again. But before she had a chance to decode the note, the mist letters disappeared.

"Shoot! I missed it." Lucy pushed on the door again, this time with all her strength. "Forget it! I'm not strong enough."

Lucy turned away from the door and looked up toward the full moon overhead. "What are we going to do now?" she asked Scratch as she knelt down beside him. Lucy closed her eyes and sighed. She tried to remember exactly what the letters were—the ones that made no sense. Her brain finally kicked in: yeK ruoY esU. The letters were backwards.

"Oh, I get it!"

Lucy stood up, took in some cool night air, and breathed it back out onto the invisible glassy surface. She rewrote the letters in her own mist and read them again—backwards this time. Yek ruoy esU. "Use your key!"

7

Lucy removed the golden key from her neck and scanned the door for a place to insert it. Floating on the invisible veneer was a small gold pair of bat wings with a keyhole in the center. Lucy carefully inserted her key and turned it in the lock. Gently, she pushed the invisible door open, stepping through with one foot, followed by her entire body. Scratch trotted in after her.

On the other side, they were no longer in the same woods that surrounded her country neighborhood. It was a very different type of forest. The grass was shoulder high and enormous pine trees with trunks the width of her whole house towered overhead. The moon peeked through the lower branches and highlighted huge drops of dew on the

tall blades of grass. Lucy walked forward, drawn to the pale light between the trees. After a short distance, the forest opened up to reveal an absolutely giant full moon, hanging heavy in twinkling stardust.

Lucy stopped and looked out over a green meadow that stretched far and wide beneath her, dotted with violet blooms as far as she could see. She stood, feeling small, near the edge of a rocky cliff with this beautiful otherworldly place before her. She gasped at the sight of it all. The mammoth lavender moon, suspended above, made everything else below it look miniature and as if it had been sprinkled with lunar glitter. In the distance, an ancient stone castle stood anchored in the valley floor and clouded in mist.

"Lucy," a voice said from behind her.

Lucy thought it sounded like Snow's voice, and she turned toward the sound to see exactly who had said her name. She jumped with surprise when she found all four VamPixies standing—full sized—right behind her. Lucy backed away from them.

"Oh, my gosh! You're huge!" she blurted out.

The now super-sized VamPixies with their extra large glistening wings giggled at her discovery.

"What has happened to me?" Lucy asked. "You didn't tell me I was going to shrink?"

Scarlet laughed. "Well, you never asked what happens on the other side of the door! And besides, did you actually shrink or did we grow? Hmm, that's something to consider." She laughed again, this time even harder.

Lucy hesitated and then chuckled with her. She wasn't sure what else to do, or what to think about Scarlet's statement. She did feel different. In fact, she felt stronger and more alive. She noticed that her skin was tingly, and as she ran her hands through her hair, it felt softer than usual and bouncier, as if she had just had a haircut and had it styled curly for fun.

Although Lucy was concerned about what exactly had happened when she slipped through the secret door, it didn't stop her from wanting to begin a new life of adventure. Lucy was about to become a VamPixie with new friends and magical powers. The fact that her friends were also mystical beings was a bonus.

Now that the VamPixies were real girls, Lucy was able to see them in a different light. They still had wings encrusted with sparkles and beautiful clothes and gorgeous long locks, but they looked different to Lucy. Their skin seemed to glow with a cool light, which she guessed was because they were supernatural beings, and there was a hint of sadness in their eyes that couldn't be concealed by their cheerfulness.

Lucy was somewhat relieved to see that the mini-VamPixies had grown into something a little less perfect than their tiny selves appeared to be. When they were tiny, Lucy hadn't noticed that Aluna had a gap between her two front teeth, or that Snow had a trail of pinkish freckles across her nose and cheeks that contrasted her nearly transparent skin. Being normal size revealed a large scar down Scarlet's arm, and as Opal began to chew on one of her fingernails, Lucy saw that her other paint stained hand was bleeding from the nail bed and had dripped onto her skirt. They weren't flawless after all. They were real girls just like her.

Lucy did observe that the girls before her looked to be slightly older than she was. They had somewhat curvier bodies than her lanky, straight one, and their faces were a bit more like girls that she knew in the eighth grade, rather than sixth graders like she was. Lucy tried not to let the age difference, or the fact that she felt a little uneasy being the only non-vampire-pixie among them intimidate her.

Opal was biting her nails nervously, but stopped when she realized that Lucy was watching her. "Are you ready to go to VamPixie Castle?" Opal asked Lucy, as she hid her hands behind her back. A drop of blood dripped down Opal's cheek.

When Lucy saw the blood, she wondered if there might be fangs under her sparkly lips. After all, things had changed when she crossed over to their world.

Snow quickly stood up from petting Scratch, took Lucy's hand and said, "Yes, I think we should go now."

Lucy pulled her hand away and tentatively mumbled, "Okay," as she scanned all four of the VamPixies' mouths for pointy teeth.

Scarlet asked with a toothy grin, "What are you looking for?"

"Um, nothing!" Lucy said quickly, looking back through the giant forest for the door to escape if she needed to. She was relieved when all four VamPixies smiled at her with a wide, fake grin, showing her their fang-free smiles.

Whew, no fangs. Lucy smiled back at her friends.

Scarlet glared at Lucy.

Snow logically explained, "We believe in peace, not violence. We grow sugar beans that give us the energy we need so that we don't need to feed on blood. VamPixies are a different breed of Supernaturals. We evolved beyond bloodlust centuries ago."

"Besides, blood tastes awful. I mean, that's what they say anyway," Aluna said, and scrunched up her nose.

Snow asked, "Okay then, are you ready?" And she pointed to the castle in the distance.

"Yes, I think so," Lucy replied. She wondered how were they going to get there?

"Oh wait, did anyone secure the passage?" Snow asked. "Lucy, you must always use your key to lock the door behind you. We don't want strangers coming through."

"Sorry. I'll go lock it," Lucy assured her and stepped back toward the archway of vines and roses she had come through.

As she neared the invisible door, a strange feeling came over Lucy once again. The fine hair on her arms stood up as she turned the jeweled key in the lock. It's just because of the cool night air, she thought, as a chill ran through her. She ignored her instincts and went back to her new friends who were waiting in the moonlight.

"Let's go," Lucy said.

Snow and Opal each grabbed one of Lucy's hands in preparation to act as her sky ride to the castle. Lucy held them tight, squeezed her eyes shut and squealed, as their lavender wings began to flap and all three girls gently lifted off of the dewy ground and into the air. With a VamPixie on each side and her arms outstretched to each of them, she felt like a baby bird being carried by its mother. Lucy finally opened her eyes and saw Snow and Opal smiling back at her.

"Breathe!" Snow called out to Lucy.

"You're safe! We promise! You can trust us," Opal added.

Lucy let the air out of her lungs that she had been holding in since her feet left the ground. At the same time, her belly relaxed, followed by the muscles in her arms and legs. Lucy laughed as she floated through the starry sky with her magical new friends, a glittering landscape below and Scratch close behind.

They landed lightly in a meadow of wild flowers that surrounded the castle. Lucy was surprised to find out that the grass was nearly waist tall and the flowers were bigger than her head. The castle, still a walk away from where they stood, looked like an ancient palace, towering over lush gardens. Emerging from the wildflower meadow was a path of tiny crystal stones leading towards it, and over this was an arbor of trees that were dripping with lavender flowers. As they walked, a shower of petals floated down like snow around them.

It was lovely! It was the most stunning and magical place Lucy could have imagined. She wondered if she was in a dream, as one flower skimmed her cheek, but it felt too real to be one.

They walked and walked through the quiet night beneath the endless falling blossoms, until the canopy of trees finally opened up to a garden of roses that had bloomed in a rainbow of colors. Perfectly trimmed bushes edged their walking path and twinkled with tiny lights, as if stars had descended on them to rest a while.

In the center of the rose garden was a fountain with a stone sculpture of a flying VamPixie woman with giant bat wings. The marble woman's face was looking towards the large crystal moon that she held in her upturned palm; her small moon reflected the light of the real one above. A spicy rose perfume wafted through the garden. The smell was so intoxicating that Lucy wished that she could lay down right there and go to sleep.

The flowery scent followed the girls as they left the garden and walked through another maze of starlit bushes before the castle grounds were revealed. The massive stone structure was made of grey and white stones that glistened under the moon's glow. It reminded Lucy of European castles that she had seen in history books from the library with fluted columns and archways and pointed tops that crowned the highest towers, all surrounded by beautiful countryside and gardens.

"Is this VamPixie Land?" Lucy asked.

The girls looked at each other and burst into laughter at her question. After they settled down, Snow answered proudly, "This is Xiemoon."

"Key-moon," Lucy whispered back to herself, vaguely remembering it from a line in the VamPixie Promise.

Flanked by tall pillars and topped with matching statues, the front entrance was grand and inviting. The stone sculptures were similar to the one of the flying woman that they had passed in the garden, except their wings were spread, and they looked down like guardian angels on anyone who might pass under the wood carved sign between them. 'VamPixie Castle, Est. 1620' was chiseled into the sign and under the writing was a circle with an eye inside.

Lucy stopped. She recognized this circle-eye carving. This was no 'déjà vu' moment. No, Lucy knew for certain that this was the same symbol that was on the Xietu talisman that she found in the cave back home.

But what did it mean and why was it here in Xiemoon?

Lucy didn't know why this symbol was on the VamPixie Castle door, but she did know that she needed to pay attention to it. After all, that talisman had brought her nothing but bad luck back home, and seeing it here made her wonder if the VamPixies were actually evil vampires with an elaborate plot to drain her of her blood once they got her inside. She thought she trusted them, but this made her question whether she should.

"Okay, stop! What is that?" Lucy blurted out, pointing at the double doors before her.

"What's wrong?" Aluna asked, watching Lucy's feet cement to the earth.

Lucy looked at the group of winged creatures before her. "Why is there an eye on your door?"

"That's the symbol of the Key-two," Aluna said.

"Xietu?" Lucy asked.

"Yes, the Xietu is very meaningful to us. The eye inside the moon is a symbol of VamPixie strength," Aluna said. "Our power comes from the immortal moon. She allows us to see the truth. She guides and protects us. It's on the door as a sign of peace and also protection against anyone who may want to harm us."

"The Xietu is good then?" Lucy asked, silently wondering if her fears that the talisman was bad luck were unfounded.

"Yes of course!" Snow answered. "It's good and powerful."

"I guess I should have kept it," Lucy mumbled to herself.

"Kept what?" Scarlet asked, looking intrigued by Lucy's curious discomfort with The Xietu.

"Oh never mind. It's nothing," Lucy said, trying to drop the subject. She wasn't sure if she should tell her new friends about the secret Xietu talisman that she found back home, or not. They might want it back, which would be impossible since she didn't have it anymore. She wondered if the VamPixies already knew about that she found the Xietu. Did they think she had it? Maybe they were planning to take it from her. They seemed to know things that they shouldn't, like that Scratch was sick. But why haven't they asked me about it?

What did it all mean? Lucy stared at the symbol while she considered her options. Maybe she shouldn't trust the VamPixies so easily? After all, Aluna keeps talking about the taste of blood—she must have tried it before. And they seem so mysterious and secretive. Even if they are a pixie blend, Lucy wasn't certain that she could completely trust the vampire part of them.

Despite the fact that she did not like keeping secrets, she decided not to tell her new friends about the Xietu she had found for now. She needed to know if finding the talisman was an accident, or if she— Lucy—really had been chosen to have it, and if the VamPixies had another reason for bringing her to Xiemoon other than friendship.

The giant eye that marked VamPixie Castle's entrance disappeared as the heavy wooden doors parted to reveal what was inside the stone exterior. Lucy and Scratch followed the VamPixies into the golden glow of flickering candles that lit the great room, or "parlor" as her new friends called it.

The expansive room was draped in lavish fabrics, as each of the tall windows that lined it was adorned with brocade cloth. An enormously long wooden dining table with a crystal vase full of white roses and a sparkling chandelier above it was formally set with six sets of unmatched, yet unique china.

Each chair at the table was different from the next, resulting in an artful hand-carved collection of natural, painted, and metallic antique seats.

"Wow, this place is so beautiful," Lucy said, as she ran her fingers down the crackled walls, over the antique grand piano, and across the velvet backed chair. A seating area of plush antique furniture was arranged around a massive, white marble fireplace that contained a roaring fire. Sculpted into the center of the stone mantle were roses and the letter V with a pair of bat wings to the side. Lucy could not have dreamed up a more magnificent room or romantic setting.

Scratch, who had followed Lucy inside, made himself at home, and plopped down on one of the oversized pillows in front of the fire. He grinned, quite happy to have found his spot, sitting atop a cushion trimmed in gold and tassels.

"Come and warm up by the fire," Opal said to Lucy.

Lucy smiled in agreement and walked over to the fireplace. Her eyes were drawn to the old black and white photos in fancy silver frames that were arranged on the mantle. Although she didn't recognize most of the people in the photos, Lucy did see a familiarity in the faces belonging to the young girls in them, and wondered if they were the same VamPixies she was with now. Curious, but not wanting to appear nosy, Lucy turned her back to the photos and the fire and took in her surroundings. There would be plenty of time later to ask questions.

Enchanted by her new friends, Lucy noticed that their beautiful wings had lowered down their backs and now hung softly like a jeweled train on a fancy gown. The clothes that they were wearing on this night were even prettier in full-size than their miniature clothes and were so much more glamorous than her own simple wardrobe of jeans, sneakers and a sweatshirt. Like their lovely home, their clothes looked as if they were made from scraps of the past, mixed with the present and put together in this VamPixie-way that Lucy would never think of doing. She tried not to stare.

"I love your outfit," Lucy said when she noticed that Scarlet had caught her examining her fashion.

"Oh thanks, I designed everything myself," Scarlet said, tugging on the hem of her velvet jacket. "Hats and shoes can tell you so much about a person," she said, pointing to the sage green beret on her head. "This one was inspired by a hat I saw a girl wearing in the streets of Paris."

"I've never been to Paris," Lucy admitted.

"We go there now and again. You know, when someone needs our healing services. And I always try to do a little window shopping for ideas while we are there," Scarlet said.

Lucy wondered how many other VamPixie dogs, cats, and possibly even people there might be around the world.

If her friends had gone to Paris to save a life, certainly they had gone other places too.

Aluna interrupted. "I'm hungry. Would you like some tea and something to eat? We must keep up our energy!" And without waiting for a reply, she sashayed off to the kitchen.

"Aluna is an expert pastry chef. Her culinary creations are edible art," Opal said.

Snow, Scarlet, and Opal, sat down at one end of the long dining table. Lucy followed, and Aluna returned momentarily, rolling a silver cart full of petite cakes and other gourmet goodies that she quickly placed on the table in front of them. It looked like fancy sweets from a restaurant to Lucy.

"Bon appetit," Aluna said and took her seat at the table. "Would you like some sugar bean tea?" she asked Lucy.

Lucy nodded yes, because she thought she shouldn't refuse, and watched Aluna pour the steaming liquid from a large ceramic teapot, decorated with finely painted flowers. Lucy hesitated to drink the tea until the others had some, partly because she had never tasted sugar bean tea and partly because she wanted the others to drink it first, just to make sure it was safe. She wanted to completely trust her new friends, but Lucy needed to be certain that the VamPixies intentions were true before she let her guard down.

The girls began to sip from their fancy china cups. Lucy cautiously followed their lead. The milky sweet tea tasted of cinnamon. She watched them each take a chocolate cupcake from the crystal cake platter in the center of the table. Lucy put one on her plate too. It was a beautiful little cake, expertly decorated with glittery pink frosting that was sculpted into flower and butterfly shapes. Lucy continued sipping and watching every move they made.

As Aluna parted her lips to take a bite of her cupcake, Lucy gasped. She thought she saw—no, she definitely saw two pointy teeth protruding beyond the straight line of Aluna's pearly whites.

Snow must have been watching Lucy watch Aluna, and noticed that Aluna's fangs were showing and that Lucy had seen them, because she cleared her throat and widened her eyes at Aluna.

Lucy put down her tea. "Um, I think I need to go home now," she said, and quickly stood up from her chair.

"Wait, it's okay," Snow said. " I promise. As we've told you before, we don't bite people, or suck blood, but our fangs do extend when we eat foods with a lot of sugar. After we finish eating, they will retract again. See, watch what happens."

Snow took the last bite of Aluna's cupcake away, just as she was about to bite into it. Aluna's fangs popped back into alignment with her other teeth almost immediately.

Aluna smiled, and said, "Sorry if I scared you, but we really can't help it. One of the hazards of being VamPixie is that we have natural instincts that we can't control—not completely."

Scarlet and Opal giggled and covered their mouths with their napkins, looking a little ashamed.

Lucy sat back down. She had to trust that what Snow had said was true.

The VamPixies devoured their cakes and reached for another, licking their sparkly lips. It was obvious to Lucy that they were trying to be polite and hide their fangs in front of her.

Lucy finally picked up her cupcake and took a bite. It tasted even better than it looked and she filled her mouth again and again. One bite tasted like strawberry, one like chocolate, and one sort of marshmallow-like. She savored the last bite and looked up from her empty plate, ready for another, but Opal had just snatched up the last cake from the platter. Lucy knew that this was Opal's third cupcake, because there had been enough for each girl to have two, and the VamPixies had already gobbled down seconds.

Five large bowls of fresh strawberries drizzled with chocolate syrup and a tower of whipped cream were the final course of this sweet meal. There was even a cookie in the shape of a bone for Scratch that Aluna placed on a plate next to Lucy. Scratch jumped up on the chair to dine with them.

"We LOVE sweets!" Opal said as she poured herself more tea. "But we can't have too much or we go a little batty!" She laughed nervously and exposed her fangs.

Lucy forced a smile, so she wouldn't look worried.

"What I mean is that we get a bit crazy if we eat too many sugary treats! Everything in moderation!" Opal said.

Now that Snow, Scarlet, and Aluna had finished their cupcakes, their fangs had retracted, and Lucy let out a sigh of relief. But Opal didn't stop eating. She shoved nearly half of that last cupcake into her mouth at once. Lucy's eyes widened. Opal's whole body had begun to light up and glow from within, as if she were a lamp and someone had just flipped the on switch. The look on her face was one of pure delight!

"Opal! Stop eating that now! You are glowing!" Aluna said.

"Oh! Oops, I must have gotten carried away! I'm so sorry." Opal was talking a mile a minute, her lips still covered in frosting. "Here, you can have this one." And she put the half eaten pastry back down on her plate and shoved it toward Lucy. Opal reached for her teacup for one last swallow to wash it down, but as she hastily grabbed the cup, it shattered as if it had crushed under her strength. The tea spilled all over Lucy's lap.

"Sorry Lucy, I'm such a klutz!" Opal said apologetically to Lucy as she tried to clean up her mess.

"See, this is what happens when we overdo it!" Snow said, throwing up her hands and glaring at the illuminated girl next to her. "Glowing is not to be taken lightly!" she said, obviously irritated by Opal's sugar high.

"What happened to 'everything in moderation,' huh?" Scarlet said.

"It's okay...really," Lucy dried her jeans with her napkin. But inside, she wondered what Opal could do with all that strength.

Opal quickly changed the subject. "Would you like to go flying now?" she asked Lucy.

Lucy could see that her fangs had disappeared, so she said, "Well, okay, but how can I fly without wings?"

Opal gestured for Lucy to follow her. "There's a pair in my room," Opal said, and ran quickly up the grand staircase that led to the second floor. "Follow me!"

Lucy chased behind her, lured by the prospect of getting her very own sparkling wings.

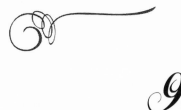

9

Opal threw open the double doors to her room, which slammed opened on account of her super-strength, and rushed inside to find the spare wings for Lucy.

Lucy came in behind Opal, stopped near the foot of her ornate silver bed frame and admired the artwork that filled nearly every square inch of the space that wasn't used for sleeping. There were beautiful paintings and drawings of flowers, the VamPixies, and the castle. Portraits of other faces that Lucy didn't recognize, charcoal studies of animals, and more paintings of flowers filled the walls behind those. It looked as if there was a lifetime of artwork piled up in her room, along with several easels with works in progress and a large table, piled with charcoal sketches, glass jars of paints, a wet palate, and several brushes standing in murky water.

"These are really great," Lucy said as she squeezed past a wet painting towards the antique wardrobe that Opal was standing near. "How long have you been painting?"

"Seems like forever, but I'm not really sure. I like to paint the things I see and the people I know from my past and present," Opal said, as she looked around the cluttered space.

And up Opal went, gently floating up to the tall peaked ceiling.

"What are you doing?" Lucy called to her.

"Looking for your wings," she answered. "Oh, there you are!" Opal drifted toward a darkened corner and back down to the floor. She touched lightly on the wooden planks, now holding a furiously fluttering pair of wings.

"These will have to do for now. They will be your practice wings so that you can get the feel of it.

The pink wings were a smaller version of the glistening butterfly-bat wings of the VamPixies. In fact, they looked more like a moth's wings to Lucy. This wasn't exactly what she had hoped for. Besides this, there were strange worm-like tendrils that hung from the center where, she guessed, the two wings would join the potential wearer's back.

"Don't worry. They're really sweet. These were my training wings, and now and again they fly back inside to visit," Opal said, as she placed them on Lucy's shoulders.

Lucy felt a tickle, followed by a mild suction, sort of like when she used to stick her little sister's hand on the end of a vacuum hose to make her giggle. That was all it took for the little pink wings to magically stick there, instantly calmed by the connection to another human.

The calm didn't last long, though, as Lucy's moth-wings seemed to react quite violently to her. The next thing she knew, those powerful little appendages were dragging her all over Opal's room, knocking over paintings and tipping over lamps. Lucy was a rag doll on a roller coaster ride, and the room was quickly becoming a disaster area. Paintings were knocked over and paint splashed all over the floor.

"Help!" Lucy screamed.

"Hold on Lucy!" Opal answered and chased down her wild wings. She held the pink appendages tightly and brought Lucy down gently to the floor. "I guess I should have told you how to ride them first. You have to tame them or the first ride can be a little bumpy."

"That's an understatement!" Lucy said.

Opal giggled. "These little guys are very excitable. They didn't mean to hurt you. Don't worry. They'll calm down now that the initial shock of human connection has passed."

"I hope so. What do I do now?" she asked.

"You must learn to be a part of your wings. Your wings are a living, breathing animal, just like you. Let's start by breathing deeply and slowly."

Lucy closed her eyes and began to breathe calmly, her chest rising and falling slowly. Almost immediately, she could feel the wings start to soften. "How's that?"

"Good, now reach back and touch them, but keep breathing," Opal instructed as she pushed the buzzing wings open, flat to Lucy's back, so she could reach them.

The surface of the wings was soft and slick, like how Scratch's puppy fur used to feel when he was a baby. Lucy smiled. The wings gave one last vibrating flutter before they relaxed completely for their new human.

"I think we're friends now," Lucy said.

Downstairs, Snow was entertaining Aluna and Scarlet while they waited for Lucy and Opal to return with her new training wings. She was playing a classical song on the piano and singing very beautifully, as Scarlet and Aluna waltzed around the room together laughing and spinning, arm in arm.

Lucy stopped half way down the banister and listened to Snow finish playing her song. Her mind drifted off with the music, admiring how each one of the VamPixies seemed so sophisticated and talented. Scarlet was fashionable and creative. Aluna was a wonderful chef, Opal a talented artist, and Snow an accomplished musician.

In comparison, Lucy thought her own talent—playing the guitar, was only marginally good, at best. She liked to play, but she was technically still a beginner. She did think that she was a pretty good writer though; at least that's what her mom used to tell her when she had the time to listen to the stories she concocted. Her mom always said that she had a "creative mind." But Lucy's stories weren't nearly as fantastical as what she was living right now. She couldn't possibly come up with anything as amazing as Xiemoon or characters as interesting as VamPixies. This was exciting stuff, but stuff that could never be told, not even to her mom or her friend Jax.

Lucy descended the final steps of the staircase into the parlor and wondered if she would ever go back home. Xiemoon was so much more fun than her life on The Outside. True, being an Honorary VamPixie was great, but becoming a full-fledged VamPixie would mean she could stay forever.

Scarlet couldn't contain her sarcasm. "Aw, she looks so cute!" she said as she plucked the tip of Lucy's training wings.

Her wings bristled under Scarlet's touch. Lucy smiled uncomfortably and tried to ignore her, but she couldn't help feeling like the dorky kid who still had training wheels, while all the cool kids had big girl bikes.

"The moon awaits us," Aluna said. She pushed open the door and they all stepped out into the starry night.

Lucy followed behind the VamPixies as they left the castle. She watched as their big beautiful wings, that had been lowered when they were indoors, rose up again and readied themselves to fly. Her small ones looked puny and awkward next to theirs, but Lucy tried not to feel silly in them and followed her friends out into the night.

They formed a circle on the castle lawn and stood hand in hand. Snow led Lucy to the center of their circle and said, "Lucy, we welcome you to Xiemoon, and to our circle of friendship."

Lucy nervously replied, "Thanks," in acceptance.

Together the VamPixies held up their Secret Sign. Lucy did the same and followed along as they began to recite the VamPixie Promise. Lucy tried to remember it all, mumbling through the parts she had forgotten. Luckily, nobody seemed to notice.

Friends forever, we stick together,

As sisters of the night.

With pure hearts and healing hands,

There will be no bloody bite.

Peaceful guardians of Xiemoon,

We promise to do right.

And listen to the wise Moon,

She is our guiding light.

VamPixies Forever!

They pointed their electric peace fingers at Lucy. She felt a strange heat come over her as the VamPixie's fingers began to glow and a lightning bolt of electric energy created a field around her.

"What is happening?" she whispered, as her heart raced and her glittery training wings began to flitter again, in fact, her whole body felt as if it were buzzing with an ecstatic energy that she had never felt before. Lucy felt like she could do anything.

"You're going to fly," Snow said to Lucy.

"Okay!" Lucy said.

Lucy grinned as her wings began to hum. She felt like they were a part of her now, and she was ready to let them teach her how to fly. Her wings were buzzing feverishly. But as her body began to feel lighter and the heaviness in her legs began to lift, Lucy stopped breathing and clenched every muscle in her body. She stretched her toes to the earth in an effort to touch it, but the ground had moved from under her feet.

"No, stop! My wings are too small to hold me!" Lucy started to panic and scream.

Snow, who was floating right next to Lucy, began coaching her on what to do next. "It's okay! You can relax now. Trust the wings!"

"I can't!"

Snow reached out and grabbed one of Lucy's clenched fists. "Trust yourself, Lucy!"

She had no choice but to trust her wings and let go. There was no time for doubt or worry at that moment. She had to use every ounce of the limited faith that she had in herself to make sure she didn't dive head first to the earth and break her neck. And so Lucy closed her eyes for a second, un-fisted her hands, and remembered how terrified she was to dive into a swimming pool for the first time. She could hear her mom standing at the pool's edge, guiding her, "Arms over your head. Tuck your chin. Now, go!"

And so she breathed in deeply, raised her arms, relaxed her body, and began to swim through the air. She pushed back the air with her arms and fluttered her feet. Lucy soared off on her own as if she had been able to fly her whole life. She soon realized that flying was effortless, and she soon stopped her swim technique and floated weightless in the sky. Lucy felt so light, yet powerful, like she imagined a real VamPixie might feel. All her fears disappeared as she flew around the castle and blissfully circled the trees for practice.

Because Lucy was in training, she stayed behind while the VamPixies took their nightly flight to the moon. She practiced her new flying skills and explored the castle grounds with Scratch.

The night air smelled like spicy vanilla around the castle. Lucy and Scratch flew over the fruit and vegetable gardens and the strange willowy trees on the hill behind the castle. They stopped to pick one of the long red pods that hung from these trees. Lucy guessed that this was the sugar bean tree, because when she broke open the fruit, the inside was filled with crimson-colored, glittering granules. Lucy licked her finger and dipped it right into the sugary substance, tasting cinnamon and vanilla and pure sweetness all mixed together like the tea she had earlier. The exotic fruit's sugar made Lucy's cheeks feel flushed.

Next, they flew along a stream that led them to a pond filled with water lilies, and landed on the stone bridge that arched over the still water. On the other side of the pond was a big red barn with stacks of hay piled high and a meadow where six bat-winged horses grazed quietly. The giant moon above them cast a lavender hue over the dreamy landscape, and the misty valley flickered with lunar light. Before heading back to the castle, Lucy paused in the soft glow and thought about how lucky she was to be in this lovely place.

But then she caught sight of a shadow of a different type of creature, lurking just beyond the barn and this idyllic scene. This dark creature had a very large wingspan and a long snake-like neck. It hovered low in the air and then disappeared into the forest that surrounded the valley. A gang of other winged shadows, which had emerged from the dark forest, followed it. Whatever these menacing looking creatures were, Lucy didn't want to stick around to find out.

"Come on Scratch, let's go," she whispered.

"Where are you going?" a voice whispered from behind her.

Lucy jumped and ran from the voice that startled her, lifting into flight.

"STOP! Lucy, it's me!"

Puzzled by the familiar voice, Lucy stopped in mid flight. "Me who?" she asked as she turned toward the voice.

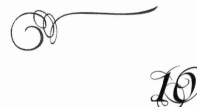

Jax was standing right there on the bridge in Xiemoon.

"Cute wings," he chuckled. "Halloween isn't for a few months."

"What are you doing here?" Lucy asked and floated back down to the bridge below her. "How did you get in?"

"Well, I kind of followed you. I heard Scratch barking from your barn, and I...I let him out. That's when I saw his wings, and you came out and ran into the woods, and I really just wanted to make sure you were okay. And then I slipped inside the door before you locked it," Jax confessed. "Man, this place is crazy!"

"But you can't be here. Xiemoon is supposed to be a secret. I wasn't supposed to tell anyone. Oh, my gosh, the VamPixies are going to be mad," Lucy said.

Before anything else could be said, a shrill call shattered the quiet, originating from the shadowy beings that had just spooked Lucy a moment ago. This was no bird. This cry sounded like it had come from a creature that was much fiercer than she or Jax were equipped to handle.

"Follow me!" Lucy yelled as she took a running start, and leaped faithfully into the air, her trusty little wings keeping her airborne. Jax sprinted behind her and Scratch followed as the ominous dark wings circled above them. Lucy led Jax toward the castle, heading specifically for the VamPixie Eye on the front door that she hoped would protect them from the winged beasts overhead.

Lucy nervously watched out for Jax, who was lagging behind his two flying friends. Luckily, the creature that was chasing them retreated quite quickly when they reached the rose gardens that surrounded the castle.

"What the heck were those things?" Jax said as they reached the castle entrance.

"I don't know, but they're gone now," Lucy answered thankfully. "And now you have to go before my friends come back."

"Go where?" he asked.

Irritated, she said, "Home, duh! You have to go home Jax."

Hurt by Lucy's demands, Jax hung his head and turned. He stopped and asked, "Aren't you coming? I'd say you're a little cuckoo if you want to stick around after that."

"No. I'm staying," Lucy said. "It's way more exciting than home, and in case you haven't noticed, I can fly."

Jax sighed. "You're going to make me find my way back in the dark with that thing around, probably hunting for its next prey? That's so considerate of you. And how would you suggest I get out of here anyway? You locked the door. Remember?"

"Oh, I guess you're right," she admitted. Lucy considered her options for a moment and said, "How about if I hide you until the morning and then I'll sneak you out early? VamPixies probably sleep all day."

Lucy motioned to the entrance of an underground cellar behind the castle. She opened the door and they stepped inside. Scratch's glowing wings lit the way down the narrow hallway toward the dark, cold room ahead. Just outside the opened door to the cellar was a small table with a glass oil lamp and some matches on top. Jax lit the lamp and carried it into the long room, lined with shelves, which would be his home for the rest of the night. The oil lamp flickered, golden against the jars and bottles stacked along the walls, full of colorful liquids and herbal concoctions. There were leaves and twigs and dried berries in some, and others contained feathers, and sparkly stones.

Jax tried again to change Lucy's mind. "Have they given you some kind of insane pills to make you want to stay here? I don't get it. It's dangerous!" he warned.

"It might be dangerous for you—a mere mortal, but I am going to become a VamPixie and learn magic and stuff like that," Lucy argued, motioning to her training wings. "Besides, my new friends are nice, and they saved Scratch. He was going to die you know."

"I thought I was your friend."

"You are my friend." Lucy realized that she had just crushed his feelings. "But Jax, I really want to do this. I don't want to go home. Please, just do it for me," Lucy pleaded.

"Guess I'll see you in the morning then." Jax grimaced and turned away.

Lucy rushed down the passage to find the girls, calling back to him, "See you in the morning!"

With each bittersweet step away from her friend, she moved toward something that Jax couldn't comprehend or be a part of. At that moment, all Lucy wanted was to become a VamPixie. As crazy as it sounded to Jax, sparkling wings, immortal friends, and a secret life, were her salvation from a life she wanted so desperately to escape.

Back inside, Lucy sipped her sugar bean tea in the parlor with the VamPixies, and worried silently about how she was going to get Jax back to The Outside. She didn't like to keep secrets from the VamPixies, but she couldn't tell them that her friend was stowed away in the basement either. If she introduced him to her friends, she would jeopardize losing her new friendships and her real VamPixie wings, even though it wasn't her fault that Jax had followed her to Xiemoon. She didn't want the VamPixies to think that she had broken her vow of secrecy. No, definitely too risky. So she silently plotted to wake up early and escort Jax out before any of them even knew she was gone.

"What time is it?" Lucy asked, hinting around to see if anyone was planning to sleep that night.

Aluna answered as she poured herself more tea, "I don't know. We don't really pay much attention to the time."

"Is it past your bedtime? Don't you know that vampires stay up all night and sleep all day?" Scarlet laughed.

"Oh right," Lucy said, "you can't go in the sun."

"Yes, we can," Aluna said. "We rise in the afternoon, before dusk. VamPixies like to get a little bit of sun on our wings before it gets dark again. The sun enhances our sparkle."

"Yes, a little sunshine is good for your spirit," Snow added. "It's not good to live in darkness all the time."

"My mom would be pretty mad if she knew I was still up," Lucy said, instantly feeling stupid after she said it in front of her more sophisticated friends. Obviously, they could stay up all night without getting in trouble, and they could eat dessert at any hour. Nobody was around to tell them what to do.

Then out of the corner of her eye, Lucy saw a person floating across the balcony that hung above the castle parlor. She turned to see a woman come down the stairs in a long flowing robe and a glittering crown of jeweled red roses that were in striking contrast to her silver hair. Her wings, hanging low on her back, were pure white and angel-like. As the noble looking lady came closer to Lucy, she could see that it was an older woman, yet ageless at the same time. There was something about her that still looked young, even though her hair had lost its color and her pale skin had wrinkled around her bright eyes. Lucy thought that if there were such a thing as a VamPixie queen, this person would definitely be it. No introductions were necessary. This had to be Salu, High Priestess of Xiemoon.

Lucy slowly stood up from her chair at the dining table to greet her. Salu remained completely silent until she was standing right in front of Lucy. She looked down into Lucy's green eyes with her blue-grey ones, and Lucy felt her body start to tremble in fear. At first, Lucy thought she might know about Jax, but then Salu's gaze softened, and one corner of her mouth turned up, and then the other followed, resulting in a lovely warm smile. Lucy stopped shaking and smiled back hesitantly.

"You must be Lucy?" Salu said. "I understand that you would like to be an Honorary Member of the Secret Society of VamPixies. Do you think you are ready for that responsibility?"

"Um, sure. I think so. Yes, I am ready," Lucy said.

"Well then, let me explain what you must be able to do in order to earn your VamPixie wings. Do you know The VamPixie Promise yet?" Salu asked.

"Sort of."

"Then you will need to memorize it, but the meaning is what you need to understand. It's quite simple really." Salu explained:

> Friends forever, we stick together,
>
> As sisters of the night.

"We value friendship and loyalty. By repeating the VamPixie Promise, you are promising to become part of our sisterhood," Salu said.

> With pure hearts and healing hands,
>
> There will be no bloody bite.

"The magic that you will learn will be of great value and power, but it must never be used with harm in mind.

Our magic is used for healing, and sometimes protection, but never for violence. VamPixies are committed to keeping the blood lust of the vampire in of us extinct—we do not bite living things. That kind of violent behavior is not acceptable in our world.

Peaceful guardians of Xiemoon,

We promise to do right

As a keeper of Xiemoon, your duty is to protect it from anything or anyone who threatens it.

And listen to the wise Moon,

She is our guiding light.

VamPixies Forever!

"The moon is your guide in Xiemoon and beyond. Always listen to the moon. The moon's light lives in your heart, and her knowledge is in you."

Now Lucy didn't fully understand this moon thing yet, but she nodded and said, "Um, okay. I'll do it." What a lame response that was, she thought, but she couldn't think of anything else to say right then.

Salu smiled and said, "Good. I shall leave you now." And she turned to leave.

Lucy blurted out, "Wait! When will I get my real wings?"

"When you are ready to have them." Salu stopped and answered sweetly. "Good evening girls." She floated back up the castle stairs as mysteriously as she had appeared.

Completely baffled by Salu's uncommitted response, Lucy sat down to a plate of sugar bean cookies. She ate slowly, lost in her own thoughts and questions about the secrets of Xiemoon, her new friends, and now Salu, who was the most mysterious of them all.

Weren't there any tests that she had to complete, or perhaps an obstacle course, she wondered, as she sipped the sweet tea. "When you are ready to have them" was not the answer Lucy was looking for.

Then there was Jax. Although she wasn't happy that he had snuck in the secret door behind her, Lucy worried that he might be cold and hungry, all alone in the cellar. She felt terrible, hiding him away, but what else could she do?

Tired and full of cookies and tea, Lucy flopped down on a giant velvet pillow by the fire next to Scratch and yawned. Scratch looked perfectly cozy, as his glittery wings acted as a blanket while he snored away. Lucy stroked his head, as she thought about home. It was her first night in Xiemoon. Had her mom noticed that she was gone yet? Would she worry when she woke and found that her daughter was not in her bed? She hadn't given it a thought until now.

While Aluna, Scarlet, Snow, and Opal sat down next to Lucy and talked about spells and cultivating herbs found in

Xiemoon, Lucy's eyelids grew heavy. As much as she was interested in learning everything there was to know about VamPixie magical practices, she drifted off to sleep.

That night, she dreamt about home.

In this dream, Lucy saw herself standing before the secret door, still in Xiemoon, but about to unlock the passage to The Outside. She inserted her key and opened the door. As she crossed over Xiemoon's border, the sticky tendrils that held her wings to her back, released themselves, propelling her forward. Scratch barked at the bat-moths as they disappeared into the night.

Lucy listened to her footsteps as she crunched along the path toward home, and Scratch flew ahead, his wings illuminating the path through the woods of Crystal Creek.

This dream felt so real to Lucy, like she was actually there. She thought it strange that she was aware that she was dreaming.

Lucy crept in the back door to her house, tiptoed up the stairs, crawled into her bed, and pulled her patchwork quilt up over her nose. It felt as if she had never left her bed. What seemed like minutes later, Lucy got up and readied herself, anticipating a typical morning, followed by a mind-numbing day at school. She walked to school with Jax, endured the day, and afterward her mom, Mara and Scratch were waiting for her outside her classroom. Lucy's mom commented on how healthy and energetic Scratch seemed to be. Lucy tried not to giggle.

After school, she did her homework, and practiced her guitar. She could hear Mara screeching over her slow plucking. Next, Lucy helped her mom make dinner, ate, and did the dishes. For desert, she had a bowl of leftover blackberry cobbler with ice cream. It made her tooth hurt, as ice cream often did, so she rubbed some of her little sister's tooth gel on the tooth to stop the ache.

As Lucy's toothache subsided, she realized that she had choices and could make things happen in this dream. She was definitely dreaming, yet she was in control of her actions. Normally when she dreamed, she felt like she was watching a movie in her mind of random events, but this time, she was a decision maker in this dream, just like when her tooth hurt and she made it feel better. This was strange, and it had never happened before.

Lucy decided that she was going to take advantage of it.

Ever since she had learned about the powerful Xietu symbol, she knew she had made a terrible mistake in thinking that her secret talisman was bringing her bad luck. She never should have returned it to that cave. This was her chance to get it back.

"Scratch, let's go find that talisman," Lucy said, petting the sparkling skins on his back.

After her mother had gone to bed, Lucy opened her bedroom window and let Scratch fly down to the ground below to meet her. She slipped on her shoes and snuck down the stairs, grabbed a flashlight and headed outside.

With no time to waste, Lucy started to run behind Scratch toward the cave. She needed to get that jeweled necklace back in her possession and take it back to Xiemoon before her dream ended.

Lucy was now convinced that the note inside the talisman's box was meant for her. It was her destiny to return this sacred symbol back to where it belonged. Surely if she brought the Xietu back to the VamPixies, they would be grateful and probably give her a real pair of glittering wings and invite her to stay in Xiemoon forever.

Under the dark canopy of trees, Scratch's lavender glow led them to the cave's entrance. Lucy turned on her flashlight, which turned out to be very dim—probably due to old batteries. She shined the fading light over the vines that concealed the cave's entrance. The purple flowers had died and fallen off the vines, leaving a thorny mess of sticks and browning leaves. She ducked under them and went inside.

Lucy moved her light across the dirt wall, looking for the hole that contained the fabric-wrapped Xietu talisman. Before she had a chance to find it, her flashlight went dark. With no light, Lucy traced the bumpy surface of the cave with her hands, feeling every sharp rock and windy tree root. Finally her fingers poked inside an empty space.

No. This can't be, Lucy thought. She picked up the flashlight, shook it, pushed the switch on and off several times, and finally managed to get a few more seconds of light out of the failing batteries. It was enough to prove that the hole where the talisman should have been was empty and the talisman was gone. Could it have fallen out? She crawled around, feeling her way along the dusty floor, but found nothing. She sat down in the dark, feeling Scratch next to her. "This is awful! The talisman is gone, and it's all my fault."

But Lucy didn't have time to waste sulking about where the lost Xietu had gone. She needed to get back to Xiemoon before her dream ended and complete an equally important task—return Jax to The Outside where he belonged. She had left him there when her dream started, but he also walked to school with her this morning in this dream. Lucy wondered how that was possible if he was still in the cellar under VamPixie Castle? For that matter, Scratch was in Xiemoon too, asleep on a pillow in front of the fire, and so was she.

"I don't know what's going on, but we have to go back to Xiemoon now," Lucy said to Scratch. "We have to go find Jax."

Lucy stepped outside the cave and into the moonlight. "The door to Xiemoon is this way," she said to Scratch, pointing down the dark path. She ran behind Scratch until they were back at the everlasting wall, which was parted by an arch of red roses and vines. Lucy unlocked the invisible door, stepped through with Scratch, and made sure that this time she locked the door behind them.

Her dream must have ended here, because Lucy opened her eyes to see Scratch on the pillow next to her, snoring. She quietly slid out from under the heavy silk duvet that the VamPixies had laid over her to keep her cozy. The sun was bright, trying to get in behind the heavy drapes that kept it dark inside the castle. Lucy opened the front door and crept outside. Her eyes watered as she squinted to avoid the bright light. She guessed that it must have been at least noon, because the sun was directly overhead. The VamPixies would probably be asleep for several more hours. Lucy shaded her eyes with her hand and walked around to the back of the castle where the cellar was.

The heavy cellar door creaked when Lucy pulled and shoved it open. She descended the stone steps and entered the cool dark hallway that led to Jax's hiding place. She could see a soft light at the end of the hall. "Jax, you here?" she whispered. Lucy traced her fingers along the damp stone walls, expecting to hear Jax answer from the cellar. But instead, all she saw was the flame of the oil lamp on the shelf, casting shadows on bottles of potions that lined the walls of the storage room.

There was no Jax. He was gone.

"Jax, where are you?" she asked a little louder. "This isn't funny! Come on out."

But there was no response, only the faint sound of footsteps coming from the back of the room. As the footsteps got louder, Lucy tried to remain calm. They footsteps finally shuffled to a stop, right in front of her.

Then Lucy felt a light breeze blow gently on her hair and face. She felt like the footsteps and the hair blowing were taunting her to react, but she didn't move. Although she felt like screaming, she stood absolutely still for what felt like several minutes. Goose bumps formed on her arms.

It was completely silent down in that basement aside from the sound of her own breathing—or was that someone else's?

"Aaaah!" Lucy felt something poke her shoulder.

"It's me!" Jax laughed.

His voice even sounded like he was right there next to her, but he wasn't anywhere to be seen.

"Where are you?"

"Right here!" Clammy fingers grabbed Lucy's hand.

"Stop it! You're creeping me out!"

Jax laughed again.

"Why can't I see you?" Lucy asked perplexed.

"Well, I got really hungry, and while I was looking for something to eat, I found this little jar of stuff that said 'Invisibility Serum!' Now the VamPixies will never know I'm here, and you won't get in trouble. That way, I can stay and make sure you're okay. I'm a genius, right? It was kind of tasty too, by the way."

"Genius? Urgh! I can't send you home invisible! I wonder if there's an antidote for it somewhere in here."

Lucy held the oil lamp and walked up and down the narrow isles of the long shelf-lined room, reading the labels on each and every jar of herb and bottle of brightly colored liquid. Most of the labels were a jumble of letters that didn't appear to be English; Teofrat, Xiekind, Rotenbut, Lukiu. There was nothing that looked like it would cure Jax.

After reading each and every label, Lucy leaned against the wall at the end of the room. "Now I have to tell the VamPixies that you're here," she said to her friend. "Come on. You've ruined everything!"

She tried not to be mad at Jax, but all she could think about was how much trouble she might be in. She feared that the VamPixies would be so upset with her that they would not accept her into their Secret Society, or give her the big sparkling wings that would make her a real VamPixie. This was bad.

The invisible boy followed Lucy outside into the sparkling, sun-drenched landscape and inside the front entrance to the castle, which was still quite dark inside.

"Sit down at the table and don't move," Lucy commanded Jax. "We have to wait for the VamPixies to wake up. I don't know how long that will be."

Time moved slowly. The grandfather clock in the corner of the room made each second feel like an eternity. Its tick-tock mocked Lucy as she paced around the room considering the best ways to tell her new friends about her stowaway friend. There was no easy way, she decided, just the truth. At three o'clock, a ding-dong-ding sounded.

Lucy sat down next to Scratch in front of the fire and waited, dreading the inevitable confession to come. Jax stayed put on the dining chair, his invisible form undetectable, aside from the depression in the chair cushion. As they waited, Lucy watched the food that had been on the dining table in front of him slowly disappear.

At 4:09, Opal, Snow, Scarlet, and Aluna slowly began to rise and filter downstairs to begin their morning rituals.

"Breakfast?" Aluna asked.

"Yes, please!" Opal answered.

Scarlet went around the room and pulled open the long draperies that covered each tall window in the parlor. As the golden sunshine streamed in and bathed the room and everything in it in light, Scarlet's lavender skins seemed to nearly disappear, leaving this immortal girl practically wingless. All that was left of her former appendages was a shadow of her wings and billions of tiny sparkles.

Lucy watched Snow, Aluna, and Opal come into the light. Each of their wings looked like they had become holographic imprints of their previously solid forms. She looked back at her own training wings to see that they too had become a glittery ghost of the ones that she had worn the night before.

As the VamPixies stood in the sun and stretched themselves into the day, the starry light that glinted off of their wing jewels seemed to brighten. Lucy had to shade her eyes to avoid squinting at them. They didn't seem to mind that their wings had changed. It must be normal, Lucy thought, anticipating a discussion about a different kind of invisible thing—Jax.

There was no use avoiding the inevitable any longer, so Lucy stood up, walked over to the chair where Jax was sitting, and announced to the sparkling room, "I have something to tell you. There's someone here with us now that you don't know about. I...I hid him in the cellar last night."

"What? Who?" Scarlet moved in close to in front of Lucy, demanding answers.

"Him? You brought a boy here?" Opal asked, dropping the stack of china plates on the dining table with a loud clank.

Aluna silently pointed to a leftover cookie floating in the air. Chunks from the cookie were progressively disappearing until finally it was completely gone.

"I'm sorry, but I thought if you guys found out, you would be mad and kick me and my little pink wings out of here," Lucy said. "This is my friend Jax. He followed me to the secret door and snuck in behind us. I promise, I didn't know."

"Lucy, you still broke the vow of secrecy," Snow said. "That's not right. You knew he was here last night, and you should have said something then. Salu is going to be furious with you when she finds out about this, and she'll probably be mad at us too for allowing this to happen!"

"Lucy didn't mean for this to happen," Opal said. "And maybe Salu doesn't need to find out. We could keep him hidden, until we reverse his invisibility and send him back to The Outside. That way, Lucy won't get in trouble, and neither will we."

"She lied!" Snow said. "That is inexcusable. I don't want to get in trouble because of her and I certainly don't want a liar to be an Honorary VamPixie. It goes against our code."

"Me either," Scarlet added.

"You shouldn't be mad at Lucy. She didn't know that I followed her in the door," the invisible boy said.

Aluna put down her plate of pastries on the table in front of Jax. "Yeah, it wasn't her fault. Besides, she couldn't just send her friend home invisible."

"But she should have told us last night," Snow argued. "Besides, we can't fix his invisibility problem. Have you forgotten that Edge stole the last of invisibility antidote from us? We would have to get it back from the Moonsprites and that could be dangerous."

"Wait, don't I get a say in this?" Jax asked.

"NO!" all the girls answered in unison and continued their argument.

"Well, it might be kind of fun to go and mess with Edge," Scarlet said.

"Who's Edge?" Lucy asked.

"He's the Moonsprite's leader. He's a big jerk and he smells bad too," Aluna said and curled her lip to show her distaste for him.

"So let's go get it back!" Scarlet said, fake punching the air.

"Alright, I'm in," Aluna said, making the "V" sign with her hand. "As long as I don't have to touch him."

"Me too," said Opal. "You are outnumbered, Snow. Come on, she needs our help. They both do."

Snow folded her arms over her chest. "Remember, the Moonsprites are an unpredictable tribe of boys. They can't be trusted."

"Why not?" Jax asked.

"Actually, the Moonsprite boys aren't that bad, it's Edge. By the way, his real name is Edgemont." Aluna stopped to laugh with the others before she continued her story. "He was always a relatively harmless troublemaker, until one foggy night he drank the invisibility serum and disappeared for weeks. Finally, he emerged from the forest with permanent fangs...and they weren't from eating sweets. Edge claims that his fangs grew because he feeds on the blood of small forest animals, which is frowned upon, but unfortunately not against the VamPixie laws."

"He's disgusting," Scarlet said.

"Does he bite humans?" Jax asked.

"Well, he can't bite other VamPixies or mortals. That is against the Xiemoon code and unless wants to be banished from Xiemoon society and imprisoned, he wouldn't do that. He's just a powerless bully that feeds on helpless squirrels." Aluna said.

Opal chimed in, "But, he could get power from Xienite Mountain, you know."

Snow explained, "Xienite Mountain is an ancient and special place to us VamPixies, full of knowledge and powerful healing energy. VamPixie legend says that if you take the Life Essence Crystals from the caves of the mountain, you will gain great power. It is even said that the Life Essence Crystals can bring back our mortality. It is against VamPixie law to touch or take these special crystals from Xienite Mountain, but we think that Edge has stolen some of these and has used them to develop his fangs, amongst other things," Snow said.

Aluna added, "Well, we think maybe he's also getting help from…"

Scarlet stepped in front of Aluna, interrupted her, and said, "Or maybe his fangs grew back because he starved himself of sugar beans. That could also cause it. He is awfully skinny you know." Lucy wondered why Scarlet cut Aluna off in mid sentence.

"Wow, he sounds like a scary guy! Is he the only guy in Xiemoon who has the antidote? Why can't you just make some more?" Jax asked.

"It's one of the few herbal tonics that we need the simiroot for, and it has become extinct here in Xiemoon," Snow explained.

Opal changed the subject, enthusiastically proclaiming, "We can handle him. Right girls?" They all nodded except for Snow. "Snow, are you in?"

Snow looked around at her friends and finally said, "Only because I'm outnumbered and because I want to make Edge understand that his evil ways will not be tolerated in Xiemoon. He deserves to be put in his place."

"Don't worry, it will be a piece of cake!" Aluna said to Lucy as she flexed her muscles. "Now, I'm hungry, and breakfast is ready."

"He needs to go back down to the cellar," Snow ordered, pointing to the door, "Before Salu sees him. Tonight we'll go to the Moonsprites fortress and get the antidote back."

"Tonight," Jax protested. "How about now? I'd like to get out of here as soon as possible."

"That would not be possible," Scarlet snapped. "We can't fly during the daylight." She pushed her hand through Opal's wing, to demonstrate why that wouldn't work.

"Our transparency is a weakness that we haven't been able to overcome," Snow said.

"Why don't we talk about this over breakfast? Come on Jax, you must be hungry!" Aluna grabbed the air until she found his arm, smiled in his direction, and guided Jax toward the door. "We'll have a picnic outside so we can sun our sparkles."

"What about Salu?" Lucy asked with concern.

"Don't worry, Salu is busy moon meditating," Aluna said. "We usually don't see her until our lesson time. Anyway, you're invisible. She'll never know he's here."

"Don't underestimate Salu," Snow said. "She would smell him if he got too close."

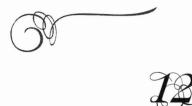

The VamPixies, Lucy, and her invisible problem, gorged on a decadently sweet picnic breakfast outside in the rose garden. Lucy had gotten used to the sudden appearance of fangs when sugar was around, but she hadn't warned Jax. She heard Jax gasp when the girls began eating.

Above, the moon was still full and hanging dimly over VamPixie Castle, despite the sun's bright appearance. When the VamPixies spread their sparkling holographic wings to soak up the sunshine, Lucy was reminded of how wimpy her training wings looked in comparison. She couldn't wait to earn her real ones, and she hoped that this whole mess she was in with Jax hadn't screwed up her chances of getting the real thing.

Between bites of chocolate fudge muffin and banana cake, Lucy asked hopefully, "So can I still go to magic class today?"

"Yes Lucy, we are in this together now," Snow said in a forced tone that made it obvious she was annoyed by Jax's presence. Snow flashed a fake, fangy smile in Jax's direction. "After breakfast, he will go back to the cellar and you must come to VamPixie Prep as planned, or Salu will know something is wrong. We'll have lessons and then steal back the antidote later on tonight, after dark."

Lucy replied quietly, "Oh, okay," and continued eating, trying to ignore the pastries that were mysteriously rising into the air and disappearing rapidly next to her.

The invisible boy asked again, "So, why do your wings disappear?"

"It's very complicated. Remember when we explained that we are a blended tribe?" Snow asked Lucy who nodded yes.

Snow stopped and looked to Aluna, Opal and Scarlet. "Should we explain?" she asked them.

The VamPixies huddled together and whispered amongst themselves.

Snow eventually stood up and perched herself atop a large stone seat next to their picnic. Opal and Scarlet crouched down behind Snow quietly.

Snow began, "A long, long time ago in Xiemoon, before there was such a thing as VamPixies, there were vampires and pixies—or Xie folk as they were sometimes called. The Vampires, being the mean and ugly and horrible monsters that they were, were not only destructive to our land, but began to hunt down the tiny winged pixies as a source of food."

Scarlet and Opal jumped out comically from behind Snow. Scarlet, acting as the vampire, twisted her red locks around her fingers, crept behind Opal, bared her teeth, and spread her transparent wings as if they were a cape that she was about to wrap around her victim. Opal smiled sweetly and batted her eyes, as the innocent pixie, and pretended to plant seeds around them. Using her magical abilities for effect, she raised her arms up towards the giant moon and wildflowers magically unearthed themselves and bloomed. Lucy and Aluna giggled and clapped enthusiastically at their antics.

Snow ignored them and continued talking. "Apparently, our pixie blood tasted sweeter than any bunny or duckling around, no matter that the Xie were little people who didn't have very much blood to give in the first place."

For dramatic effect, the pixie magically shrank to her miniature size. She looked just like she did when Lucy first met her on The Outside.

Snow continued her story. "The tiniest bit of Xie blood tasted better to a vampire than all the blood from any animal or mortal human being, even bunnies. Mortals are great for quantity, but the quality is sometimes undesirable."

Following the storyline, Opal, the pixie ran through the tall grass, cowering in fear as Scarlet, the huge vampire stomped behind and snatched up her prey. The sky darkened around them, and the vampire flashed an exaggerated smile, pretending to bite into the pixie's pale little neck. The pixie flailed under her captor's grasp and dramatically fell limp in the vampire's hands.

Clearly tired of being upstaged by her friends, Snow folded her arms over her chest and waited for the dead pixie to resize herself, and the horrible monster to take her bow and sit down. She began again, "So instead of leaving Xiemoon to find their prey, the Vampires began to snack on pixies, thereby turning the pixies into vampires and then keeping them around for slaves or eating them whole when they grew tired of them."

Aluna, who was itching to be a part of this VamPixie play, stood up, brushed off her blue tunic, and picked up where Snow left off. "And eventually, there was only one pixie left who had not yet been turned into a vampire. That pixie was Salu's father, Dr. Angus Saige. He was very clever. He cast a secret spell over the vampires that cannot be broken to this day." As Aluna told of the spell, she reached out for what looked to Lucy to be a handful of air, but when her hands opened over the vampire's crimson hair, tiny sparkles drifted from her hands. And she ended with, "That spell destroyed their bloodlust, and their fangs became dull and useless."

Lucy lay her head down on the grass, contemplated everything she learned from this VamPixie drama, and finally asked, "What happened to Dr. Saige?"

Snow replied, "He died because he was not turned into an immortal VamPixie like us. He was already ninety-nine years old when the Xie killings began, and Salu was already well into her later years when she was bitten and made immortal by the vampire king, that she later destroyed. Luckily, Salu and her father were able to stop the horrible violence and the vampire's evil ways before Dr. Saige passed away naturally, as the last true Xie folk left in Xiemoon. "

Lucy interrupted, "Whoa, whoa, whoa! What happened to all the vampires who turned the pixies into VamPixies?"

Smirking with satisfaction, Scarlet said, "They're gone. Salu lured them out from their creepy cave at Xienite Mountain, where they lived. It appeared to be dark outside, but it was a trick. Dr. Saige created a solar eclipse with his magic, and right when Salu lured the vampires out into the dark, her father commanded the moon to uncover the sun and expose the vampire's dark hearts to the bright light of day!"

Opal giggled and added, "I would have loved to see their faces when they realized that it wasn't really dusk, but an illusion that shattered their immortal souls! Before they could scream in terror, the sun's rays crystallized their forms, which fell to the ground as tiny amethyst sparkles."

"Aren't they pretty?" Scarlet asked as she motioned to her glittering wings.

"So that's how you became VamPixies." Lucy thought out loud.

"Well, that's how the VamPixie tribe began," Opal answered.

Jax's voice said, "How many VamPixies are there?"

Opal thought for a moment and said, "Well, there are about thousands of us here in Xiemoon. We are all from Xie blood, all VamPixies technically...but a long time ago our tribe split up into several smaller tribes because there was fighting and a struggle for power in Xiemoon. Now, there are VamPixies, Moonsprites, Shadow Girls, and lots of others, which live, hidden away in the vast Xiemoon forest. We are all very different, with different abilities, and we live separately by our own tribal rules. But every creature in Xiemoon must follow the VamPixie laws of nonviolence that were established by Dr. Saige."

"The Shadow Girls are strong and sneaky. They can camouflage themselves in any dark place and not be seen. The Moonsprite boys use technology to build things and bring them to life, but they aren't that great at magic. And we are master herbalists and healers. We have a strong connection to the earth," Aluna said proudly.

Snow interrupted Aluna to finish her story. "And with his powerful magic, Dr. Angus Saige saved Xiemoon from the evil vampires that were threatening it, and helped this new tribe of blended beings—the VamPixies–to live peacefully again. Sr. Saige is no longer alive, but he passed on his knowledge, his spell books, and the Xietu to Salu. She has vowed to carry on his legacy." Snow smiled.

"The Xietu?" Lucy asked. Her interest peaked when she heard mention of the mysterious symbol again.

Aluna explained, "It's an ancient VamPixie talisman, infused with Angus' spell and inlaid with the precious Seizerstone from Xienite Mountain. The Xietu gives its wearer special abilities. The fate of Xiemoon is held in the hands of whoever possesses it."

"I think I understand now," Lucy said, knowing this had to be the very same secret Xietu talisman she had found in The Outside.

Why didn't Salu have the Xietu, Lucy wondered? Why was it left in a cave if was so important? Why would someone have chosen me to return it to Xiemoon? Lucy couldn't let the VamPixies know that she had done something as stupid as return the Xietu to the cave because she thought it was bad luck. They would probably be really upset if they found out, and they might decide not to help Jax, or they might not make her an Honorary VamPixie after all. No, she couldn't tell them yet, even though she knew it was risky and wrong to keep secrets from them. But the stakes were high, and she figured that she could find the Xietu and return it to them before her secret was exposed.

Jax interrupted. "Excuse me, but you never answered me. Why do your wings disappear in the daylight?"

"Like we said, true vampires can't go out in the sun at all, or they'll disintegrate," Aluna said. "Because we are half Pixie, we can be out in the sun, but our magic doesn't work, and our bat wings are very weak."

They were interrupted by a bell, which sounded three times, and prompted the VamPixies and Lucy to rush down the garden path to the cobblestone building where spell advisory and magical guidance would be given.

"Meet you in the cellar!" Lucy called out to Jax.

13

The inside of the small school they called VamPixie Prep smelled of herbs and old books. One wall was packed with well-worn spell books from floor to ceiling. Lucy shivered as she ran her fingers along the spine of one leather-bound book that was titled: Volume I, Xie Spells. Attached to the bookshelves were long ladders that could roll on wheels to whatever magical book you might want to reach. Between the bookshelves were tall stained glass windows that invited the last light of the day inside and spilled vibrant color across the whitewashed wood floor.

There were five antique desks made of wood and wrought iron arranged in a semicircle, with a podium at center front for Salu to stand while advising her students. Lucy sat down in the center chair and waited for Salu, who floated in behind them.

"Let's start with a lesson in Vishphixie." Salu directed, as she took her place in front of them. "Vishphixie is our own secret Xie language that only we can speak and understand. It is an ancient language that we use only to invoke magic," she said, looking at Lucy.

Salu turned and stared intently across the room at a vase of white rose buds that sat on a table next to an open book of spells. In a hushed tone, she spoke a word that Lucy had never heard before. The white roses became red and slowly bloomed.

"What did she say?" Lucy whispered to Opal, who was sitting next to her.

"Xiekallory," Salu explained.

"Huh? Can you repeat that please?" Lucy asked.

"Key-ka-lo-ree," Salu said slowly.

"What does it mean?"

"Xiekallory turns your thoughts into reality. If you think in your mind that you want the red flowers to turn white, visualize the transformation, say Xiekallory, and you can make it happen. But you must think it with strength and conviction. Use your will. If any part of you is not 100% committed to turning those flowers back to white, your magic will fail."

Lucy asked, "What is my will?"

Salu replied, "Your will is your personal power and inner strength. It's quite simple really. When your mind is strong enough, you can make anything a reality. 'Xiekallory' spoken correctly, is the second thing you need to set your magic in motion."

"Now Lucy, lets see if you can make the flowers turn white."

Nervously, Lucy stood up and moved in front of the vase of flowers. She visualized the red flowers in her mind and the color white and tried to remember exactly how to say it. "Key-la-la-ko-ree!" The girls giggled behind her. Nothing happened.

"Now, let's try again. Take a deep breath, clear your mind so that you are only thinking about the color of the flowers and say the word as I do. 'Xie-kallory.' Are you ready?"

Visualize, Xielalalory, Xielalakory—no, Xiekallory. Got it. Lucy was determined to do it right this time. She planted her feet, stared even harder at the flowers and sternly said "Xiekallory!" Nothing. The room was completely silent.

Again, Lucy closed her eyes, listened to her breath, and began to feel her own inner strength move throughout her body, as if she had awakened some new form of electricity that flowed up from the earth and took over the cells of her being.

Lucy opened her eyes and calmly said, "Xiekallory." Her whole body began to tremble, and then she felt like she was heating up from the inside. She stared intently at the red flowers that slowly paled to pink. But she had never felt this kind of power before, and it scared her. Her heart was racing and she felt like she couldn't breathe, much less continue to concentrate on turning the flowers white. Lucy gasped for air and sat down.

"Can I take a break?" Lucy asked.

Salu handed Lucy a glass of water. "It's okay. You'll get used to it."

"But I feel like I can't control it," Lucy said.

"You can," Salu said. "You're a natural, with such a strong will. Trust your own strength, Lucy."

"Okay," Lucy said.

Standing before the pink bouquet, Lucy closed her eyes again. She concentrated even harder on the color white and whispered the Vishphixie word several times to herself before letting loose an unexpected sneeze. When she opened her eyes, the flowers were still pink, but the skin on her own arms and hands had turned from a healthy bronze to bright red.

"Oh, no! How do I fix this?" She imagined that the rest of her was red too.

The VamPixies burst into laughter.

"Quiet Girls!" Salu said. "Now Lucy, you are not concentrating properly. I know you can do this."

"Well obviously I can't," Lucy said, looking down at her red limbs.

"You must, unless you want to look like that forever," Scarlet said.

"Now, breathe slowly," Salu said to Lucy. "Visualize what you want in your mind. Feel your strength. Don't fear it. You have the power to make anything happen. When you are ready, say the word."

This time, the heat that Lucy felt was more concentrated right in the middle of her forehead. She had never had a headache before, but if she had, she figured it might feel kind of like this. The pressure in her head only lasted for a few seconds, and then she felt her entire body chill and develop goose bumps. Lucy said Xiekallory to herself and opened her eyes to find that her skin was its normal color and the roses were completely white.

The more she practiced, the easier it became for Lucy. She changed the flowers back to pink and then red and back to white again. Once she understood how to use her power, Lucy mastered the tasks that were given to her quickly and easily—almost too easily. Her mind had always been sharp, but now she had found something that both excited her and tapped into her ability to focus. Lucy had finally found something she was good at, something that made her feel special. For the first time in her life, she felt strong and powerful. She wasn't just an average girl anymore. She was becoming a VamPixie.

At last, she felt that she belonged in Xiemoon with her immortal friends. Lucy had found her tribe, and she was ready to take on Edge and the Moonsprites with the VamPixies tonight.

14

The sun was setting as the girls left VamPixie Prep. A pink haze covered Xiemoon and the giant moon above it. While Lucy went down to the cellar to fetch Jax, the VamPixies went inside. Snow gathered a few tiny vials of herbal potions from a cabinet in the dining room and put them into a small leather pouch that she wore slung across her shoulder. Aluna, Opal, and Scarlet discussed their plan to steal the invisibility antidote while Snow distracted Edge.

Lucy screamed, "Woohoo!" at the top of her lungs and lifted off into the night sky, following her tribe to meet the gang of boys. The Moonsprites fortress awaited them, dark beyond the jagged cliffs of Xienite Mountain, in the Desert of Stones.

Scarlet and Aluna held on to Jax's invisible hands tightly, as they flew in front of Lucy, dangling Jax between them, hundreds of feet in the air. Although Lucy couldn't see him, she did hear him scream.

It was a long journey, and Lucy soon relaxed and let the wind carry her for what felt like hours. Eventually, Snow motioned to her that they were near. They floated down silently, landing in the tall grass.

They stalked through the grass, crouching low so as not to be seen, but they soon became exposed, as the grass ended and the ground became parched, plant-less, and covered with tiny crystal pebbles. The ground glittered under the moonlight like fresh fallen snow. There were dark outcroppings of huge boulders sprinkled here and there in the vast dessert, with the Moonsprite's fortress, a jagged silhouette, looming in the distance.

Lucy held on to Jax's hand so she wouldn't lose him— being invisible as he was. The group crunched over the crystal earth and stopped in the shadow of an enormous rock, to review their plan of action.

"Cool," Jax whispered.

He was obviously not paying attention to Snow, who was drawing out their plan with a stick in the dirt. Lucy squeezed Jax's hand and said, "Shhh!" But Jax pulled away from Lucy's grip.

Snow was interrupted by a loud, hollow tone that droned through the body of the big rock they stood next to. The massive thing beside them was definitely not a natural rock. It was moving! What Lucy and the others assumed was just a boulder, was actually sheets of metal, held together with rusted bolts and washers. And it was coming to life. Giant wings lifted from its body, as the creature's tarnished copper neck snaked left and right. On the end of the neck was a fire breathing head that pushed out flames from between the silver daggers that were its teeth. The screech of machinery wailed!

"I think we're in trouble!" Jax yelled from the darkness.

First there were two and then three and then four metal beasts that rose out of their previous rock-like formations and began crashing across the dusty earth towards the VamPixies. Behind those came two more.

"Fly!" Snow screamed and bounded into the air, hovering over the Moonsprites' dragon pit. Lucy, Opal, Aluna, and Scarlet did the same, leaving Jax somewhere on the crystallized earth, amongst the fire-breathing machines.

The big rusted beasts remained grounded, Jax trapped in their midst. The VamPixies and Lucy scattered, all flying in different directions.

"Jax!" Lucy called. "Run!"

From the black silhouette of their fortress, burst the motley-winged Moonsprite boys. Their brightly colored bat wings caught the wind and left a trail of orange and blue behind them as they soared in to meet the intruders. Lucy thought they looked like dirty pirates, with ripped shirts and baggy pants tucked into tall boots. With three multi-color stripes on their faces, one under each eye, and one down their nose, this tribe looked like they were wearing war paint. Most of them had scraggly long hair, and none appear to have bathed in quite some time. Their foul smell confirmed that last assumption.

"Call off your dogs!" Scarlet yelled and flew straight up to one the boys.

"No way!" he said.

Zen held tightly with both hands to the small, rectangular metal box that controlled his rusty beast. Each one of the boys had a similar handheld device in their possession. Lucy thought that Zen's controller looked like a modified version of an iPod. How did they get a hold of this type of technology in Xiemoon? They must have stolen them from The Outside.

Scarlet lunged at the boy, reaching for his computerized control box. "Let me have that!"

"Let's go down there and fight for it," he said, dropping closer to the fiery head below him.

Lucy scanned the ground below for some sign that her invisible friend was okay while she and the opposing tribes hovered above the dragon pit.

"Come on guys," Snow said, tugging on the back of Scarlet's wings. "We just want to talk. We need your help."

"Why would we help you?" the boy said. "What do we get in return?"

"You help us, and we will help you," Aluna said. "We can get Edge off your back."

"How?" he asked.

"Shut 'em down, Zen! And we'll tell you," Scarlet demanded, pointing down to their mechanical beasts.

"All right," he sneered and touched the colorful screen of his controller. The other five boys did the same, and their dragons transformed back into the boulders they once were.

The VamPixies cautiously floated to the earth below after the Moonsprites. Lucy followed their lead, landing next to Scarlet. This seemed like the best place to be. If anything happened, Scarlet could probably protect her. She could definitely be mean when she wanted to.

Zen folded his arms over his chest and asked, "So what do you glittery girls want?"

"We want the invisibility antidote," Lucy answered.

"What do you want that for?" asked a black-haired Moonsprite.

Before Lucy had a chance to answer, Zen strolled over to her and stopped, his face too close to hers. "Who's your friend with the baby wings anyway?"

Lucy wanted to punch Zen in the stomach, but invisible Jax grabbed her hand and stopped her from lunging at him. Her face remained without emotion so that Zen wouldn't know that there was an invisible person in their midst. Lucy didn't like being controlled, but was relieved that Jax was safe.

"Where's Edge?" Scarlet stepped between Zen and Lucy.

"I don't know," Zen said. "And if I did, why would I tell you?"

"Because I am asking nicely." Scarlet moved in close to Zen, stopped a few inches short of him, and flashed a fake smile. "And I don't think that you want me to be, NOT nice."

"Go ahead," Zen said, poking her shoulder with his finger. "Show me how a VamPixie isn't nice!"

While the other Moonsprite boys laughed with Zen and high-fived each other, Lucy noticed that footprints had appeared in the dust beside Zen. Jax was definitely up to something.

"Psst, look," Lucy said quietly to Scarlet and pointed to the footprints. "Jax is right there," she whispered.

Scarlet looked back at the VamPixies and winked before she turned around and said, "Girls, are we ready to show these geeks a thing or two?"

Lucy didn't know what the wink meant, but she figured that it must be part of their plan.

But before the girls had a chance to do act, down went Zen's grubby pants, baring his skinny little legs and grungy underwear. And when he bent over to pull them up, the invisible Jax must have pushed him, because he fell to the ground. He lay on the dirt, his lip quivering as if he were about to cry. They all laughed at Zen, the Moonsprites included.

"That's what you get for making fun of a girl!" Jax said.

"Who did that?" Zen yelled.

"Our secret weapon! Come on, get up," Scarlet said as she stretched her hand out to Zen.

Zen refused to take her help, but quickly pulled up his grimy pants and stood.

Snow took over the negotiations. "Look Zen, we don't want to fight with you guys. We need your help. We need to get Mr. Invisible over here back to normal so that we can send him back home to where he belongs."

Opal stepped forward and asked in a coy tone, "Please, will you guys to talk to Edge and ask him for the invisibility antidote? We really need it."

Zen could tell that Opal was flirting with him. "Oh sure, I'll just ask him for it, and I'm sure he'll hand it over, after he tortures me into telling him that you are here. No. You need some leverage, something to bargain with. How about her?" Zen said, pointing to Lucy, "He'll definitely like her—if you know what I mean."

"We can't trade Lucy for the serum," Opal said. "How about if we send Jax in to steal the serum? Since he's invisible, Edge will never know he's there."

Zen agreed. "That sounds like a..."

"Stupid idea!" Jax interrupted and finished his sentence. "What will he do to me if he catches me?"

Lucy replied, "He won't. Jax, Zen's right. Edge is not going to fork over the serum easily. Besides, he won't even know you're there. I know you can handle this."

"We agree," Opal said, speaking for the VamPixies. "That's the best plan. Will you help us?" she asked Zen and the boys.

"What's in it for us?" Zen asked the VamPixies. "You know...we could really use some good food, and a lot of it."

"Okay," Aluna said, folding her arms over her chest. "How about four dozen of my sugar bean cream cakes."

"Oh, I think 12 dozen sounds more like it."

"Six."

"Okay," Zen said. "But only if Edge doesn't know we helped you. If he finds out, we'll suffer for it. Where's that invisible mortal?"

"Here," Jax said.

Lucy took his hand and led him to Zen.

"Girls, wait here," Zen said.

The girls huddled behind one of the sleeping boulder beasts while the Moonsprites flew off to their fortress with Jax under wing.

"I hope Zen and his gang are helping Jax and didn't lie to us," Lucy said. "I'm worried that they won't stand up to Edge."

"Stop worrying Lucy, Zen might be a jerk, but he would do anything for food…and to impress Opal," Aluna said as she collected crystal pebbles from the ground where she sat.

* * *

"Listen," Lucy whispered. She could hear someone walking toward them, crunching through the sparkly rocks that covered the Moonsprite dragon pit. She couldn't see anyone, but there was definitely something coming. The footprints became louder, as if someone was stomping on the ground so it would definitely be heard.

It must be Jax, Lucy thought to herself.

Aluna, Opal, Scarlet, and Snow stood absolutely still.

"Jax is that you?" Lucy asked the footsteps.

15

"**Yeah,** it's me, Jax."

"What happened to the Moonsprites?" Lucy asked the invisible figure in front of her. They were nowhere around. And Jax was being strangely quiet. Lucy felt the hairs stand up on her arms and she shivered. "Jax?"

But Lucy did not get a reply. Instead, a small vile of blue liquid with a white label that read 'Visibility Serum' appeared, floating in the air where the invisible boy stood. Jax liked to joke around, and Lucy figured that he must have been hiding it to surprise them. He was about to become visible again.

The girls stood at attention, watching as the vial lifted, then tipped, and began to empty. The invisible figure drank

the blue elixir with a loud gulp, followed by a burp, and a ridiculous laugh. Right then Lucy knew something was wrong. The Jax she knew was polite.

His invisible form began to slowly reappear, as if he were made of hot wax that was turning solid as it cooled. Starting with his feet and quickly moving up to his face, the liquid formed a solid boy.

"BOO!" It yelled. And it wasn't Jax.

Looking extremely pleased with the success of his trick, Edge laughed loud and hard, deliberately flashing his fangs at the girls and then doubling over with his arms folded over his belly. He was the only one laughing at his joke.

What a short little twerp, Lucy thought. He was a skinny wimp, with long, messy, reddish-brown hair and freckles. He wore a blue velvet coat that was way too big for him, and torn at the shoulder. As he strolled toward her, the soiled hem drug through the dirt.

Edge slithered closer to Lucy. Lucy did not back down, even though he stopped a few inches from her face and stared into her eyes. First she noticed his rancid smell and then her eyes were drawn to a leather string around his neck, which held a shiny silver pendant in the shape of a dragon. The dragon's tail was wrapped around a big sparkling crystal.

When the wiry Edge spoke, Lucy understood the fear that this creepy looking little person incited in the Moonsprites.

His voice was pure evil. He sounded like a boa constrictor that had learned English.

"If you want your little friend back, you better follow me," he hissed.

Lucy looked at her friends, not knowing what to do. She tried to back away, but he moved closer. She didn't trust Edge, especially not with those teeth.

Edge took hold of Lucy's hand. "Come on, it'll be fun."

Lucy had no choice but to do as he instructed. She worried that Edge had done something to hurt Jax. Would he try to bite her? Or worst yet, had he already bitten Jax? Lucy flew behind Edge toward the fortress, not knowing what they were going to find. The VamPixies followed.

The Moonsprite stronghold was not like the pristine castle that housed the VamPixies. Erupting from the earth was a structure unlike anything Lucy had ever seen before. It was a mish mash of metal objects built around giant boulders and crystal spears that crowned flat-roofed towers. As they landed at the entrance, a giant rusted dragon's head, which hung above two colossal metal doors, opened its fanged jaws and dropped a few fiery balls out of its mouth, which immediately fizzled out and gushed with green smoke. This was probably supposed to intimidate unwanted visitors, but the stink bombs weren't that effective.

To the sides of each door, were stacks of old television screens, which projected Edge's image as he strolled up to a metal box and a keyboard that was bolted to a dusty podium. The box front spiraled open after he tapped several keys to reveal a touch-screen computer. Edge touched a few icons and the double doors parted to expose the disastrous interior of the Moonsprite's digs. Zen and the other Moonsprites scattered like cockroaches when they saw Edge coming.

The dimly lit room was cluttered with old machine and computer parts, tools, jars of spiders and scorpions, a long red snake in a glass tank, and dusty old books stacked high in every corner of the room. There wasn't a piece of rickety antique furniture, or any surface for that matter, that wasn't covered in a layer of filth. Lucy tried not to breathe through her nose as she navigated her way through the boy's den.

Beyond the squalor, was another wall of television screens that hung over a row of what looked to be brand new computers. There was one boy, sitting alone, typing frantically in front of one of the computer screens. He didn't turn around, but Lucy noticed that his wings were smaller and less colorful than the other boys. Lucy wondered who this new Moonsprite was and again, how the Moonsprites had access to such things from the modern world. The VamPixies had none of this.

Edge cackled, "Welcome ladies!" as he walked through the squalor and leaned against the brass banister that twisted up to the tower above them. He stomped his feet down hard on each step of the metal stairwell.

Edge bowed as he swung open the door to his lair. There was Jax, red faced, hanging by his feet from a rope that went over the rafters and was tied to the bedpost. Lucy almost wished he were still invisible so that she didn't have to see the fear on his face.

"See I fixed him for you," Edge said. "He's visible again! Don't you want to say thank you? You should be grateful, you know."

"Let him go, you creep!" Lucy screamed and lunged toward Edge, her arms reaching for his neck.

Scarlet grabbed Lucy and pulled her back before she could get a hold of Edge to choke him. She whispered in Lucy's ear, "Keep your cool. We'll take him down another way."

Lucy glared at Scarlet, who was usually the one to pick a fight. She couldn't think peacefully, when her best friend was being tortured. Her body felt like it was bubbling over with anger, not only at Edge, but also at herself for failing her friend. She felt helpless to defend him. She couldn't even remember the Vishphixie word she had learned earlier that day. She whispered to herself, "Xie-something, Xie-morry, Xie-lorry, Xie-no shoot!"

Edge bounded into his messy room, kicking over piles of books and attempting to break everything in his way. He walked over to Jax and started swinging him back and forth like a pendulum. "I'm so glad that your sparkly friends came to visit me today because they have something that I want."

"What do you want, Edge?" Lucy asked.

Opal yelled, "Please, let him go!"

But then Lucy noticed that Snow was inching closer to Edge with a tiny glass vial of green liquid in her hand. While Snow snuck up behind him, Lucy kept him distracted.

"We'll do anything. Just don't hurt my friend!" Lucy pleaded. "Take me instead!"

Snow uncorked the top of the tiny bottle of green serum, and before Edge understood that he was being tricked, she shook the last drop of green juice onto his head. Instantly, little green insects emerged from the sappy drippings, and they scampered through his crazy red hair and disappeared beneath his clothes.

"I want...I want the Xie..." but Edge did not finish his demand.

First he slapped the back of his neck. Then he shook his head, and rubbed his chest and arms violently. Edge's face went magenta as he tried to remain composed, but Lucy could tell that the bugs had moved down into his pants because he had begun to slap and wiggle his legs. Everyone stopped and watched Edge squirm and shake. Seconds later, he fell to the floor and rolled around violently, scratching himself like a mad man.

"Stop! My skin is crawling!" Edge pleaded for mercy.

Snow batted her lashes, tossed her hair, and said, "Oh no, it's just a few million bugs." Then she bent down next to him and said, "You see, Edge, I accidentally spilled some of my Eau du Cootie perfume on you. It's an aromatic blend of lice, fleas, and spiders—the biting kind."

"Maybe it will make you smell better," Scarlet said. "You should really bathe more often!" She laughed, jigged a little victory dance around the writhing Edge, and invited the Moonsprites in to witness his pain and embarrassment.

Lucy loosened the noose that bound Jax's feet while Aluna and Opal helped him safely to the floor.

"You all right?" Lucy asked Jax.

He nodded. "I'm okay, just a little lightheaded from the blood rushing to my head."

"Let's get out of here," Lucy said, taking Jax's hand. The VamPixies followed them down the stairs, past the squalor, and out the door.

Opal turned back toward Zen. "Thanks."

Zen smiled back at Opal.

On their journey back to Xiemoon, Jax flew between Lucy and Scarlet. Lucy squeezed his hand tightly, as they soared through the twinkling stars and moonlight.

Everything was going to work out now as Lucy had hoped. Salu wouldn't find out about Jax, and the VamPixies still accepted her as one of them. Her new friends had proved their loyalty to her by helping Jax, and now it was her turn to return the favor and get the Xietu back for them. She owed them that.

The sky had begun to lighten, and they only had minutes to get Jax home before the dawn came and their wings faded into their sunlit holographic form. They hurried towards the entrance to the outside world, over the wildflower valley, and landed on the cliff before the forest of giant trees. They walked briskly through the tall blades of grass, toward the invisible door to The Outside.

"Wait, Lucy, we have to clear Jax." Aluna said. "Because we have to make sure he doesn't talk. Don't worry, it doesn't hurt, and he won't remember anything."

"What?" Lucy asked.

Jax backed up, moving away from Aluna. "I promise I will never tell. Just let me out of here. Seriously, you can count on me."

"Is that really necessary? We can trust him," Lucy said.

"It's for his own safety, Lucy. We have to clear his memory," Aluna said. "It'll just take a second and when you step through the passage, all will be forgotten. Xiemoon does not exist," Aluna said and placed her 'V' on his forehead. Her fingers began to glow warmly between Jax's closed eyes. "All clear." She released him from her touch.

Lucy didn't like this clearing, but understood that Jax was about to cross back over to a place where Xiemoon, VamPixies, Moonsprites, and the evil Edge did not exist. It would be best if he didn't remember any of it, including her presence there. She needed Jax to run back home and get in his own bed as if he never left it. She couldn't risk anyone finding out that she had become a VamPixie in training.

She took the jeweled key from around her neck and unlocked the door. Lucy looked at Jax, not knowing what to say. She did not like goodbyes, especially if she had to say goodbye to someone that she cared about.

When her dad moved out, and she said goodbye, she felt like she had lost him forever. Lucy didn't know when she would see Jax again, if ever, or when she would go back to Crystal Creek. To her, the only way to avoid feeling the inconsolable pain of 'goodbye' was to act like it wasn't happening.

But, Jax made a bold move that surprised Lucy. He hugged her tightly, and for what felt like a very long awkward moment.

Lucy pried herself out of Jax's arms. "See you later."

She paused and took a deep breath to stop the tears from forming as she removed the skeleton key from her neck, locked the door to the Outside, and turned to face the VamPixies.

16

That night Lucy dreamt about Jax from her Xiemoon home. The dream began as she watched herself unlock and go through the hidden door. Her training wings disappeared and she felt like the old Lucy, taking a morning walk in the woods that she and Scratch knew so well. Soon they arrived at Jax' tree house, climbed inside and sat down together on the edge of the wood plank floor. Without a word, they watched the clouds take shape, as they often did on weekends to pass the time. The wood creaked beneath Lucy as she swung her legs back and forth.

Jax was holding two wishing sticks in his hand. Wishing sticks are what Lucy used to call those dandelion weeds with the fluff on top. When she was little, she loved to pick them,

blow on the top and watch the fluffy white stuff drift up and into the air. She remembered that her mom always asked her if she made a wish.

Jax blew hard on one and then the other, loosening all the fluff and watching it fall slowly to the grass below.

"Make a wish," Lucy said.

"I did."

"What for?"

Jax answered, "That you would come over today, and we would go junk hunting in the woods. Let's go," he said smartly.

"Wishes don't come true if you say them out loud," she joked. "Besides, I'm only here in a dream Jax. It's not real. When my dream is over, I'm gone. Poof!"

"Yeah, right," Jax said.

"I'm serious. It's true. I'm actually asleep right now. When I wake up, I'll be back in Xiemoon."

Jax tossed an empty wishing stick to the ground. "Come on Lucy, quit joking. Jax got up and started down the ladder. "Follow me. I'll prove to you that you are here in Crystal Creek and not in Key-moon, or whatever you said."

"Wait Jax!" Lucy called after him.

Jax ignored her and walked faster, forcing Lucy to run to catch up to him. She followed Jax across his lawn and out his gate, down the gravel road to her driveway, and in the gate that led to her house. Scratch ran out of Lucy's house, without wings, and jumped on Lucy, as if she'd been gone forever. They walked in the house and her Mom said, "Do you guys want some lunch?"

"See, she sees you!" Jax said. "Can you see your daughter standing right in front of you? For real?"

"Yes, of course," she said matter of factly. "What is going on with you two anyway?"

"Nothing, he's just kidding," Lucy replied as she signaled to Jax to follow her up to her room. That same old creaky step mocked her as she put her weight down on it. Lucy stopped, backed up, and stepped on it again before she continued up the steps. Everything in her dreams about home was exactly how they had been in reality.

"I'm really confused, Lucy," Jax said, as he sat down on her bed and rested his head in his hands.

"I told you. I am in a dream right now," she answered. "At least I think I am."

"And you came from what planet?" he asked, throwing up his hands.

"Xiemoon."

Lucy didn't think it mattered what she said to Jax because she was dreaming. It was her dream, and it didn't exist anywhere except in her mind. To be safe, she figured that before she left the dream and woke up again in VamPixie Castle, she would erase his memory of the day, just in case, and that would be the end of it.

But at that moment, Lucy needed Jax to cooperate and help her find the missing Xietu. The VamPixies had no idea how much danger they were in, not to mention how upset they would be with Lucy if they discovered that she had discarded the valuable talisman and kept it a secret all this time. She had jeopardized their safety and she had to make it right, or her dreams of graduating to real VamPixie status would surely be over.

"Jax, I'm serious. I went to sleep in Xiemoon and woke up here. This happened to me last night too." Lucy paced around her room. "I don't know why. I just have to wake up, and I'll be gone again—back in VamPixie Castle. But right now, I really need your help. It's important!"

"My help? Why?"

"I told you already…to find The Xietu." Lucy snapped. She could control her own actions in this dream, but she couldn't control Jax. Her alarm clock ticked through the silence of that moment. Lucy unclenched her jaw and said, "Dreams are short. Before I know it, I'll wake up, and my chance to find the Xietu will be over. Please Jax, will you help me?"

"Okay, okay, calm down," he said. "So you fell asleep and woke up here. I just don't get it."

In order for Lucy to get Jax to help, she knew that she had quite a lot more explaining to do. Since Aluna had erased his memory of everything VamPixie, he remembered absolutely nothing of his time in Xiemoon; and Lucy had no choice but to tell him every detail that had happened since Scratch found the VamPixies in the woods that night. And so she did.

After hearing the long, and seemingly ridiculous, train of events, Jax shook his head and snickered. "Night one—you fell asleep, and Scratch became a VamPixie dog. This sounds like a dream to me. Then you woke up and went to school the next day. Night two—you fell asleep waiting for the VamPixies to come back, and you found the secret passage to Xiemoon. I followed you in, but don't remember anything because my brain was erased. This also sounds like a dream, right?"

"I guess, but it didn't feel like one. And wait a minute! You snuck in to Xiemoon with me, so it couldn't be a dream! I told you!" she gloated. "And that same night that you were hiding in the cellar, I dreamt that I was here at home, searching for the Talisman in the bat cave and I didn't find it. Then I woke up in Xiemoon and you were invisible, we stole the serum back, and all that stuff."

"See, even you are confused by your own story," Jax argued, "I think you've been watching too many movies."

They both sat quietly on her patchwork quilt, the sun casting squares on the oak floor from her window frame. Lucy suspected that her friend still didn't believe her. "Have I ever lied to you Jax?"

"Uh, not really. I guess not."

Jax sat quiet for a moment and then said, "Hey wait, I saw this movie once where these people could control their dreams when they were sleeping, and time stopped in their real lives when they were asleep. Do you think that this could be happening to you?"

Lucy thought for a moment and said, "I think you are a genius, Jax. Time stops when I go to Xiemoon. That makes total sense! I am living two lives and both worlds are real."

"Lucy, your reality is what you choose it to be. You should probably pick one."

"Why?" she said.

"Uhhh. This is all just too weird," Jax said as he headed for the door. "Don't you think your mom is going to figure this out?"

Lucy took hold of his arm. "Not unless somebody tells her. Now can you please come with me? I need to show you something. Oh, and can we bring your metal detector and a flashlight?"

Jax sighed. "Okay, I'll go get the stuff and meet you under the tree house."

Lucy smiled.

"Let's go," Jax said, toting his metallic treasure finder and handing off the flashlight to Lucy.

Although she knew that it was highly unlikely that the Xietu was in the bat cave, she wanted to be certain that she had searched every inch of it, and examined the cave for clues of where it might be. Maybe his metal detector could find it?

Scratch followed the pair down the sunlit path, as Lucy explained to Jax how valuable this item was to the VamPixies. She thought that if she told him it was valuable that he might be more interested in finding it. She told him about the note inside the wooden box—the note that said she had been *chosen*, and the box with the initials *C.W.* on the bottom.

"Lucy, this sounds like one of your stories. *Chosen?* For what?" he asked. "Why would someone choose you?"

"I don't know, but it could explain why all this is happening to me."

"So are you some kind of a secret super hero girl?" he laughed. "It's just a coincidence, Lucy."

"Thanks," she said, and jogged ahead.

"I didn't mean that," Jax said to her back. "If anyone could be the chosen, super hero, magical girl, it would be you."

"Whatever. It's this way." Lucy walked several paces in front of Jax the rest of the way there.

"This is it. That's the hole where I found it and left it," she said, shining a cone of light inside the empty hole in the hard packed dirt wall. She pointed to the metal detector Jax was holding. "So can you use that thing and make sure it isn't buried somewhere in the dirt. Maybe it fell."

"Okay." Jax flipped the switch on the handle and began slowly running the machine over the cave floor, starting at the back and moving slowly back and forth across the dusty earth. Lucy waited to hear the familiar beep of discovery while she looked around with the flashlight. But it never came.

"Maybe we should try outside, a little," Jax said. "You never know."

"Who would have taken it?" Lucy asked as she walked out of the cave and went toward the blackberry bushes to think while she picked them a snack. Scratch sat down next to her and whined for his share. Without gloves, Lucy was careful to avoid the thorns. "Hey, do you want some berries?" she called to Jax. She was doubtful that he was going to find the Xietu outside the cave. If someone had stolen it, they wouldn't have just dropped it outside.

"Sure," yelled Jax, and he and his metal detector moved toward the blackberry bushes. He leaned the machine on a stump and held out his cupped hand to receive the berries.

Beep, beep, beep, beep, beeeeeeep! The machine screamed. "I must have forgotten to shut it off."

Jax quickly popped the handful of juicy berries in his mouth and leaned down to flip the switch and quiet the annoying noise. He grabbed the handle and clicked it off, moving it off of its original spot, where something shiny caught the light and gleamed. Jax bent down to get a closer look at the small bobble that got his attention. "Hey Lucy, I found something."

"What?" Lucy answered and climbed out from behind the prickly limb she had been collecting berries from.

He reached for the miniature bobble, but when he lifted it from the spot it rested on; it grew larger with his touch. "Whoa!" Jax pinched the black leather string between his fingers, dangling a silver dragon pendant, which clutched a crystal faceted spear in its talons and glistened as it turned under the ever-changing light that streamed through the tall pines.

Lucy immediately recognized it.

"That's Edge's pendant," she whispered. "He was here. It must have gotten caught on the blackberry vines and ripped off his neck."

"Huh? Did you see? It grew!"

"Yes, I saw!" Lucy thought to herself—VamPixies shrink when they come to The Outside. Moonsprites must too. "It's too much to explain right now."

"And it belongs to that creepy guy who you say captured me?" Jax asked.

"Yeah. This is bad, really bad," she continued. "Edge—the one with the fangs, must have the Xietu. He's evil, and I just know he will try and do something bad to the VamPixies if he has the Xietu."

"Lucy, I want to believe you, but you're sounding kind of…well…insane!"

"I probably am," she said. "I'm sorry, Jax. I have to go. It's getting dark."

It was time to clear Jax and get back to Xiemoon.

"Jax, please hold still." Lucy said as she pressed her electric 'V' lightly to his forehead. As she waited for her fingers to start glowing with pale pink light and erase every immortal secret she had told him, she said, "Sorry Jax, but I have to do this. I'll see you in my next dream. Okay?"

There must have been some kind of was magical malfunction, because Lucy's fingers didn't start glowing as she expected them to. In fact, nothing happened at all. She closed her eyes to concentrate better. Still nothing, no pink light ignited her touch.

"This is not happening," she whispered to herself.

Jax stepped away from Lucy. "What are you doing?" he asked.

She dropped her hand and said, "Trying to clear your memory, but my magic doesn't work here. Promise me you won't tell anyone about this, Jax. I have to go and find the talisman before it's too late."

"I won't tell anyone. They would think I was nuts anyway," he yelled to her as she and Scratch started to run.

Lucy ran as fast as she could toward the invisible entrance into Xiemoon. She had no idea how she was going to get the Xietu back from Edge. All she did know was that she had to, and she needed to get through the secret door and back to Xiemoon as fast as her little pink wings would take her.

It seemed like forever that she and Scratch had been running toward the vine-covered wall that separated her two worlds. But soon enough, she could see the twinkling lights and roses that arched over the passage to her other existence. Lucy quickened her pace, forgetting that the rocky path was often wet and slippery with moss. With the door in sight, she sprinted for Xiemoon, hoping to stop Edge and recover the talisman before it was too late.

The last thing Lucy remembered before she blacked-out, was seeing the crescent moon that had made its first appearance in the evening light above her.

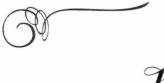

17

Lucy's body felt paralyzed as she lay still on the cold earth, but her mind was not at all quiet. She felt like she was dreaming, but this time Lucy wasn't in the dream. And what she was envisioning, she could not control.

First, Lucy saw a young girl wearing an old fashioned bathing costume, her blonde hair in ringlets and tied up neatly in bows. She was tossing a ball at the beach, which rolled to the water's edge and was pulled out to sea. She tiptoed into the ocean after the ball, laughing as a wave splashed over her bare feet. When Lucy saw a closer view of her face, she noticed the freckles across her nose. She looked a lot like Opal.

When the wave retreated, another pair of feet appeared, but this time they were standing in dry sand. The dusty feet

obviously belonged to a different girl who had coffee colored skin and wore a short skirt made of leather and adorned with brightly colored beadwork. She walked away, carrying two pails full of water that sloshed onto her legs. Her hair was braided with bright orange beads and blue feathers on the ends. The girl stopped and looked back over her shoulder. Lucy recognized Aluna's amber eyes. One feather dropped from her hair as her image faded away.

It floated into the hand of a different girl, who's back was to Lucy in her dream. Her hair was red and she wore a fancy hat. Could this be Scarlet? She dipped the blue feather into a small pot of black ink and scrolled the words *Dear Diary* in an open book in front of her. She wore an emerald ring and lace gloves that covered all but her fingers. When she plunged the quill pen back into the pot and pulled it out the second time, black ink dripped from it.

The ink drops changed the scene again, turning into silver raindrops that poured down over a gloomy city street. Lucy watched as a horse-drawn carriage rolled down the cobblestones in the distance, toward a girl in a long white coat who held a black umbrella over her head. Although Lucy couldn't see her face, she looked to be quite happy skipping through the rain alone, jumping in puddles, and soiling her coat with murky water. But then something—maybe a gust of wind—caused her umbrella to turn inside out and fly into the air, exposing her nearly colorless hair. This girl looked like Snow.

As Lucy's dreamy visions continued and more details were revealed to her, she knew that she was watching the VamPixies in real world situations. But where were their wings and why weren't they in Xiemoon?

The images kept pouring into her mind; a giant wave covered Opal and pulled her out to sea; Aluna fell onto the golden sand as a snake slithered away from under her feet; Scarlet's red hair became flames that surrounded her; and Snow lay limp in a puddle as a horse reared over her. One by one, Lucy watched them die.

Lucy felt something touching her.

"Shhh, it's okay, Honey," her mom whispered as she stroked Lucy's hair.

Lucy fluttered her teary eyes and opened them to a blurry vision of Jax and her Aunt Christina, who was holding her little sister Mara at the foot of a white bed. The stiff white covers were pulled taught across her legs. Lucy quickly realized that she was no longer in the forest, but lying in a bed in a pale grey room, and everyone was staring at her.

"Hi sweetie, I'm so glad you're awake," Lucy's mom said from her bedside.

"Where am I?"

"In the hospital, but you are going to be fine. You slipped and fell in the woods. Jax found you," her mom explained as she squeezed Lucy's hand. "Lucky Jax was wandering around in the woods with his metal detector, or you might not...I'm just so happy he was there."

"Oh." Lucy didn't know what else to say. In her mind, she was hoping that Jax hadn't told anyone about all the crazy stuff that she had revealed to him before she fell. She scanned her mom's smiling face for knowledge that she knew something. Nothing. Jax didn't tell. Jax gave Lucy a knowing look and shook his head no, just a tiny bit.

"How do you feel? You seemed restless a moment ago," Aunt Christine said, as she touched her hand to Lucy's forehead.

"I'm fine. I was just dreaming," she said and forced a small smile. She didn't want any more questions. Lucy couldn't tell them about the weird nightmares she had just woken up from. At least she thought they were nightmares.

Lucy's mom, said, "You've been through a lot, Honey, but the doctor said we have nothing to worry about."

But Lucy was worried about a lot of things—the Xietu, getting back to Xiemoon, and now the strange visions she had just woken from. She was confused about why her four friends did not appear as the beautiful VamPixies that she knew. They were mortals, dead mortals. They were not pixies from Xiemoon like Salu was. They must have been imported from The Outside, just like she had been. Why hadn't they told her this?

Jax said, "Yeah, the doctor couldn't even find a bruise on your head. No concussion."

"That's good. Now when can I go home?" Lucy asked.

"The doctor would like to keep you until tomorrow morning for observation. He thinks you might have fainted, and he wants to make sure all your vitals are stable," Her mom answered. "But don't worry, we'll stay right here with you."

Lucy couldn't think of anything much worst than to be stuck in a hospital room with everyone's attention on her. She had things that she needed to take care of.

"Are you hungry? How about if I run Jax home and pick up a chocolate milkshake for you on my way back? Christine, do you mind keeping Lucy company until I get back?" Lucy's mom asked.

"Sure," her Aunt Christine said. "We've got lots to catch up on. It's been months since I've seen you, Lucy."

When Lucy's mom, Mara and Jax left, Lucy's Aunt pulled a chair up next to the metal rail of her bed and started asking questions. "So how's school going?"

"Fine."

"Have you made new friends this year?"

"No."

"Are you still playing the guitar?"

"Yes."

The questions didn't stop, and Lucy, being tired and completely uninterested in this sort of chitchat, gave her Aunt one word answers until she stopped asking for a response.

"You know Granny Charlotte used to have these fainting episodes all the time. Maybe it's hereditary. Has this ever to you happened before?" Aunt Christine asked.

"Uh, no," Lucy said, only half paying attention to her. She was thinking about how soon she could get out of the hospital and get back to Xiemoon. She didn't care about to hear about her dead great grandmother at that moment.

"Has your mom told you much about Great Granny Charlotte—you know, the one who used to live in your house?" Aunt Christine asked.

"Oh, yeah," Lucy said. "I think Mom told me about her one time."

"Well, Grandpa built the farm house—your house, for Grandma after her childhood home burnt down. It was completely destroyed, and to this day the cause of that fire remains a mystery. Granny Charlotte always said that he built that house out of love. She loved that house, but I think she loved those woods even more," Aunt Christine said.

"Why?" Lucy asked.

"She thought that those woods were magical. But I probably shouldn't…" She paused and bit her lip. "Your mom made me promise not to tell you Granny Charlotte's stories a long time ago. Let's pretend I didn't open my big mouth!" She turned away from Lucy.

If her mother didn't want her to know about something, Lucy was definitely interested. "Oh, come on, Aunt Christine. What's the big deal?"

"I better not say. How about we talk about boys?"

"I'm not interested in boys. Please Aunt Christine! I won't tell mom that you told me; I promise," Lucy said. "Besides, I'd like to know more about my great grandmother."

Her Aunt Christine took the remote from the cart next to Lucy's bed. "How about if we watch some TV."

"No really, why won't you tell me about Great Granny Charlotte?' Lucy asked.

"Okay, well, let's just say she had a wild imagination and she got into some trouble. But she was a wonderful lady, and she always had a great fairy tale to tell us kids."

"What were they about?" Lucy asked.

"All that supernatural stuff."

"Like what kind of supernatural stuff?"

She put down the remote and said, "You know, like fairies and sprites and other creatures, which I think your mom believes are too scary for you."

"It's just a story, and I'm a little old for being scared by a fairy tale, don't you think?" Lucy asked.

"All right then, but I didn't tell you," Aunt Christina said, shaking her finger at Lucy and smiling.

This was going to be good, Lucy thought.

"Granny Whitfield's favorite tales were ones about these vampire-fairy thingees. I can't remember what she called them, but she used to scare the pants off of us kids by telling us that they lived in a magical world somewhere in the forest down by Crystal Lake."

"You're kidding, right?" Lucy laughed to conceal her interest.

"No, the problem with Granny Charlotte was that she didn't think it was a fairy tale; she believed every word she spoke."

"Oh, " Lucy said. "Did you believe her?"

"When I was little I did. She almost had your mom convinced to go with her into the forest one night to go to this secret world where her vampire-fairy creatures lived."

"Did she go?" Lucy asked.

"No, she chickened-out. But I think she always wondered if Granny Charlotte was telling the truth. Your great grandma was quite a character. She swore that her stories were real until the day she died—in a mental institution."

"What? That's awful." Lucy said. She knew that Great Granny Charlotte was anything but crazy.

"Yes, unfortunately, after Grandpa Charlie died, she got into a little trouble telling those stories. She was lonely and volunteered for story time at the library. But she didn't like to read from books, she liked to tell her own fairy tales, of course. And then she invited a few of the children from story time to meet her magical creatures."

Lucy did not show her Aunt Christine any sign that she knew anything, but inside, she smiled. "I bet that did get her into trouble."

"To top it off, she drove to their homes one night, snuck them out, and took them into the forest...without their parent's consent. The parents of these children threatened to have her arrested for kidnapping unless the family moved her into a place where she couldn't 'spread her lies' to innocent children anymore. Ridiculous! Granny Charlotte was a lovely person and completely harmless. But she sure did have a wild imagination!"

"Sounds like it," Lucy responded. "I wish I would have known her."

"Well, she claimed she knew you and Mara. She said that she could see the future, and she told your mom that she would have two girls. And she told me that I wouldn't have children, just cats."

"Seriously?" Lucy laughed.

"Yes. She predicted a lot of things that came true for me."

Before Lucy had a chance to quiz her Aunt for more information, a heavyset nurse in pink scrubs walked into her room. "Time to check your vitals. How are you feeling, Lucy?"

While the nurse took her temperature and began pumping air into the black band that squeezed her arm, Lucy thought about Great Granny Charlotte—Charlotte Whifield—C.W.? Yes. Charlotte was the one who left the secret talisman in the cave for her to find. Somehow, she knew that Lucy would be born. She really had been 'chosen' to find the Xietu.

All Lucy could think about was getting out of the hospital so that she could get back to Xiemoon. She had so many questions for her winged friends. Why hadn't they told her that they too had been mortals from The Outside? Did they know Charlotte? And did they know that Charlotte Whitfield hid the Xietu in The Outside world for her to find? Although she felt that the VamPixies were true friends, she wondered what they knew and why they had been so secretive.

"You look like you could use something to eat," the big pink nurse said, which broke Lucy free from her thoughts.

"Okay, sure, thanks," Lucy said.

Aunt Christine continued talking. "Last night I made the most divine pasta dish."

Lucy stared off into space while she spoke, consumed by her own worries. Exhausted from it all and unable to escape the constant drone of words, she closed her eyes. Eventually her aunt stopped talking, and Lucy slept.

* * *

What felt like seconds later, Lucy pulled down the silk duvet and rolled over on her lovely goose down bed. Her room in VamPixie Castle was at the end of the hall, with Snow and Aluna's rooms on one side, and Opal and Scarlet's rooms on the other. She padded down the dark wooden floors, noticing that their bedroom doors were open and beds already made. Lucy rushed down the stairs to the parlor to find them.

ALUNA was carrying a heaping plate of chocolate croissants to the dining table as Lucy stomped down the stairs and into the parlor. Opal, Scarlet, and Snow were setting the dishes for their feast.

"Good afternoon Lucy, you slept late. It's almost 5:00. Are you feeling okay?" Opal asked.

"No," Lucy said, having just woken up from several disturbing dreams where she learned that her so-called VamPixie friends were once mortals, and that her Great Granny Charlotte had been to Xiemoon. "I'm not okay!"

Instead, she grabbed the pastries from Aluna and asked, "Can one of you tell me, honestly, how you become VamPixies? I want the whole truth this time—all of it."

"Well, we all had to die first," Scarlet said flatly, as she dug her finger into the frosting of a three-layer cake. "As we've explained before, VamPixies are immortal you know."

"So every one of you is dead? Right?" Lucy asked. Her voice quivered as she spoke.

"Yes, we assumed that you would figure that part out," Scarlet said. The way she looked at Lucy made her feel stupid.

"I get it!" Lucy snapped back at Scarlet. "But you told me you were VamPixies–from Xiemoon, not ex-mortal girls from The Outside!" Lucy huffed over to the dining table, put down the platter of croissants she still held, and turned to address the girls. "You kept it a secret. Every one of you lied to me. I thought that friends tell friends everything."

"We lied to you?" Snow said, as she walked toward Lucy and folded her arms over her chest. "We didn't lie. But no, we didn't tell you everything because we don't like to talk about our deaths. That is a, well…private subject. I can't believe that you would be so upset after you hid Jax from us. Now that was a lie."

Even though Lucy knew that Snow was right, and that she, herself, still had one big secret she was keeping from the VamPixies, she couldn't let this sense of betrayal go. She continued to argue her point. "But didn't you think I should know that you were once mortal girls like me and you weren't always supernatural beings?"

"Why?" Aluna asked. She picked up a chocolate croissant and before took a bite, her fangs extended.

Lucy stared at her feet. "Well, knowing you're immortal is one thing, but knowing you are dead is…"

Opal interrupted. "That part of our history is too painful to talk about, but if you really want to know, we'll tell you." She shrugged her shoulders and flopped down at the table.

True, Lucy had seen their deaths in her dream and she imagined that reliving it would be awful for each of them.

Aluna licked the chocolate from her lips. "Does it really make a difference to our friendship if we were once mortals? We're VamPixies now. We were made immortal by Salu a long time ago."

Although she hated having secrets kept from her, Lucy was beginning to understand why they hadn't told her and her Xietu secret was beginning to fester inside her belly. And as Aluna pointed out, it shouldn't matter if they were once girls from The Outside, or if they were original Pixies who were turned. Their friendship had always been true—more than hers had been. Aside from Jax, the VamPixies were the best friends she had ever had, dead or not, and she didn't want that to change.

"I'm sorry," Lucy said. "It doesn't matter if you're dead. Friends are friends."

After the VamPixies and Lucy came together for a group hug, they said, "VamPixies Forever!" in unison.

Lucy moved away from the group. "But I can't be a VamPixie forever with you," she said. "I'll only ever be an Honorary VamPixie."

"Unless you die," Scarlet said bluntly. Then she laughed. "Gosh, don't worry, we're not going to kill you!"

But to Lucy, being Honorary meant that she would grow up and live a normal and probably average life, while her immortal friends would get to stay young girls forever. Their life seemed so ideal, death or not. If given a choice between a normal mortal existence and a magical supernatural life with her friends in Xiemoon, Lucy knew what her choice would be.

"And what if I WANT to be more than honorary? What if I want to become a REAL immortal VamPixie like you?" Lucy asked.

"Mortality is not a choice, Lucy!" Aluna said. "We didn't choose to die!"

"Don't you get it?" Scarlet asked. "Death is horrible. Trust us, if you were dead, you wouldn't want to be. It's not worth the cost."

"Well, sometimes I do…wish I was dead," Lucy said.

A teary eyed Opal said, "You don't mean that!"

Lucy looked at her friends, who glared back at her. "But I want to live here in Xiemoon forever. I belong here, with you guys. I want to be a forever VamPixie, not a fake one."

The room was silent.

Scarlet fumed toward Lucy, her cheeks nearly as red as her hair. "Would you stop being so stupid?" Her voice choked and her anger turned to sadness. "Trust me, you don't wish you were dead—not even sometimes!" Her green eyes welled up with tears.

"What about the VamPixie Promise?" Lucy asked. "You promised that we would live together forever, guided by the moon."

Snow said, "We have not broken our promise of friendship to you, and we never will."

And with that, Snow motioned to Opal, Aluna, and Scarlet to follow her toward the front door of the castle. Still weepy eyed, Scarlet turned back, glared at Lucy, and stormed outside with the others.

Lucy stood there alone, except for Scratch who was lying on a pillow by the fire. Even he turned his head away as Lucy looked to him for support.

Why couldn't the VamPixies understand that she just wanted to be one of them? Didn't they understand how important their friendship was to her? Lucy followed her winged friends outside, into the cool dusky air, to try and make them see her point of view. Clearly, they didn't know how difficult her mortal life was on The Outside. She hated school and barely had any friends, except for Jax. Her parents were divorced, and her father was a big jerk. And then there was that stupid baby brother that she did not want to know about. In Xiemoon, Lucy felt good. She could fly. She had friends. And she did not have to deal with any of her mortal problems.

Lucy flopped down on the grass under Xiemoon's lunar sky, and soaked up the giant moon's powerful energy. Her petite pink wings sparkled and twitched as she scanned the stars for Scarlet, Aluna, Opal and Snow. Lucy was positive that she wanted to become an immortal VamPixie. She wanted nothing more than to leave her old life behind in exchange for a perfect new life in Xiemoon.

"Honorary status is not enough," Lucy said to the lavender globe overhead. "Why don't they understand?"

As Lucy asked the moon this question, a strange feeling came over her. She felt dizzy, and her knees buckled, causing her to collapse. Had she fainted again? No, she felt aware and could see the moon above her. Her eyes burned a little, and the moon looked close enough to touch. But when she tried to reach her hand out to touch it, she was unable to move her body. Seemingly paralyzed, Lucy lay on the lawn, wide-eyed and aware, with only the moon in view.

The silver patterns on the surface of the moon began to swirl slowly, changing and darkening as they moved, and forming into what looked to be the skyline of a city. Then more specifically, the Eiffel Tower appeared. Lucy recognized the monument and knew it must be Paris, where she had dreamed of going one day. On the ground beneath the tower were women in fancy dresses, holding parasols, and men in suits and top hats. A girl in a long coat and a big hat with a bow that covered her face, skipped happily through the bustling crowd, carrying a bundle of books. The girl began running through the bustling Parisian streets toward a storefront with a big picture window that displayed ornate gowns, pointy-toed leather boots, and hats with peacock feathers in them.

It seemed to Lucy, that the moon had become a giant motion picture screen—all for her. Her body had started to regain its feeling and the strength to sit up and watch the show from the ground below.

The girl, in the moon's movie, hopped up the steps and walked inside the shop, past lines of fabric bolts and racks of beautiful dresses, toward a man in a suit at the back. She dropped her books on the glass counter, wrapped her arms lovingly around him and planted a quick peck on each cheek.

Then the girl quickly slipped behind a curtain and into the back room of the shop.

Tailors were cutting fabrics and seamstresses were busily sewing on old-fashioned treadle machines—like the ones that Lucy had seen once in an antique store. One of the ladies stood up from her stool, put down her work, hugged and kissed the girl, and then followed her up a narrow stairwell. At the top of the stairs, they entered what appeared to be an apartment, where the girl removed her coat and hat that had previously concealed much of her face.

Lucy's smile turned to concern as the black and white movie became tinged with colors and the young girl's hair slowly turned to a vivid red. This wasn't just a girl. It was Scarlet.

Scarlet went into a bedroom, closed the door and sat down at a desk. Her fingers carefully turned the yellowed pages of a handwritten book, filled with symbols and what looked to be formulas or recipes. That's when the images began moving faster across the lunar screen as if they were out of control. Suddenly, flames and smoke consumed the building. Lucy's heart raced, as she helplessly watched Scarlet's tear-stained face call out in desperation. As smoke began to choke her pleas for help, copper flames swallowed her body.

Lucy winced and covered her ears, as she listened to Scarlet's screams projected into the night sky. The tears began to rush down Lucy's cheeks, as she relived Scarlet's nightmare. Lucy remembered when she first witnessed the deaths of her mortal friends in her dreams how horrific they were, but this time the vision of Scarlet's death was more real and there was more to the story that Lucy hadn't seen before.

In the moon's movie, Scarlet's image lay still, consumed in flames, as a white blanket of fog descended over her body and snuffed out the carmine blaze. From this lifeless form, a ghost-like image of the mortal girl stood up from the dead one, and floated outside to the street scene below the flaming building. The ghost of Scarlet ran to the suited man, who was standing on the sidewalk sobbing as he watched the blaze. But the man did not see her presence. Her new form was not visible to him. Scarlet hugged the man, hoping to get his attention that way, but he did not respond.

Finally, she tugged hard on his collar and said, "Daddy, I'm right here."

When her efforts were ignored, Scarlet looked down at her own ghostly arms and realized her reality—she was dead. She backed away from her father, who watched the scene in horror as his wife and child burned.

Lucy's heart hurt for Scarlet. She watched the ghostly girl run again down the lively streets of Paris, but this time it was not with joy, but desperation. Scarlet was obviously terrified of who she had become, and heartbroken over what she had lost. She finally surrendered to her fate and took refuge in a cemetery. Scarlet's face looked emotionless and empty as she sat down next to a vase of pastel flowers and leaned against a tombstone with R.I.P., 1884 chiseled into the stone.

Lucy swallowed a sorrowful sob. Her questions were finally being answered by this tragic vision blasted across the moonscape.

The ghost of Scarlet looked up to see what appeared to be a star, falling from the sky. This burst of sparkling energy stopped its lightning fast decent right in front of her, and she reached out slowly to hold the magical glowing ball of sparks. When this light touched her upturned palm, her transparent form became electric and slowly began to fill back up with life, starting with her hand, moving up her arm, and finally her entire being turned to solid flesh again.

Lucy smiled as a pair of glittering pink wings emerged from the trees and fluttered around Scarlet. Just as her own had done, they latched on to Scarlet's back and became a part of her. But unlike the excitement Lucy had felt over gaining her training wings, Scarlet's face looked rather blank when she lifted into the air and followed the glowing light into the woods that surrounded the cemetery.

The images on the moon began to fade and swirl back into the silvery patterns they were before. The show had ended.

Poor Scarlet, Lucy thought. She wiped her tears and nose with her shirtsleeve.

Scratch nuzzled her from behind. "Hi Scratch," Lucy said quietly, pulling him close for a hug. He sat down beside her and dropped his head in her lap, as she ran her hand down his shiny coat.

Lucy thought about her own family. She imagined how heartbroken her mom and dad would be if she were to die and how unbearable it would be for her if she couldn't see them anymore. Even though things seemed so bad at home right now, they hadn't always been that way. She remembered how good it felt when her mom hugged her, and how, whenever she was sad, her dad used to tell her stupid jokes until she laughed. He wasn't around much any more to do that, but at least she was still alive to see him when he was. Although her little sister could be annoying, Lucy smiled when she thought of how she said her name—'Wucy.' She wouldn't want her little sister to grow up without her. Then there was Jax, who had always been a loyal friend. He was there for her when she needed him, and even when she didn't. He was sort of like family too. Lucy would miss them all terribly.

If she became immortal and gave up her life on The Outside, she would give up a lot of other things too—afternoons by the lake, birthdays, Christmas, and her dreams of being a musician or traveling to Europe, Africa and the Amazon. The sacrifices were too great. Lucy was finally beginning to understand that death and immortality were not the answers to her problems.

Her tears dripped onto Scratch's head. She wiped them off and hugged him tight. "I don't want to die."

Death is permanent. No, the VamPixie life wasn't perfect either. Maybe living a double life would be just fine. Maybe being an Honorary Member of the VamPixie tribe was the perfect life for her.

Scarlet and the others were right. She had acted stupidly.

Lucy stood up slowly, still feeling a little light-headed. "What just happened here?" she asked Scratch.

From behind, Lucy heard a voice say, "Your gift is getting stronger, Lucy."

Lucy turned to see Salu standing behind her.

"My gift?" Lucy asked.

"You are a Seer," Salu answered. "You have the Mind Sight." Salu took Lucy's hands.

"I have what?"

"The ability to see the past, present, and future in your mind. Your Mind Sight has always been available to guide you, but you didn't know what it was," Salu said, looking at Lucy.

Lucy shook her head. "I don't understand."

"On The Outside, people might call you psychic, or clairvoyant. In Xiemoon, we call it Mind Sight, because that's exactly what it is. You see images in your mind. They may seem random at first, but they're not. Your visions come because they are important, and you need to listen to them."

"Listen to who?" Lucy asked, pulling away from Salu's warm grip.

"The moon and you. You know more than you realize, Lucy, and you have the ability to see that information very clearly."

Lucy looked up at the moon and back to Salu. She remembered when she fainted in the forest and ended up in the hospital. "I thought I was dreaming before. My mom said I fainted. And I just did it again, right here."

Salu said, "Yes, I watched you fall, but you did not faint. With practice, you will gain control over your body."

"Practice? I don't understand! Didn't you see Scarlet up there too?" Lucy asked, pointing to the moon.

"No, that was only in your mind. I saw only the moon's brilliant light," Salu said.

Lucy felt as though she might cry, but blinked away her tears. "How can I tell what is a dream, or what is my Mind Sight?"

"Your visions come through the moon. Did you notice that each time you collapsed, you had been looking at the moon?"

She thought about what had happened before. "Yes, I guess you're right."

"With practice, you can become adept at summoning your Sight even when she can't be seen," Salu said, motioning to the giant moon above them. "If you can clearly picture the moon in your mind, your visions will follow."

"How do I stop this?" Lucy asked. "I don't want this!"

"You cannot stop it. Your Mind Sight is a part of you, Lucy, and you must accept it. Welcome your gift, for it is very special. As you become more adept at working with your ability, you will learn not to fall down or lose control of your body, but you cannot stop the visions. They will come when you need the information, and sometimes without any warning."

19

"Salu brought us here to live the lives we should have had," Scarlet said, as she poured the ruby colored tea into six cups.

Salu smiled fondly at the four girls that she had given a new life to so long ago—a new life as the undead VamPixies. Since their turn to immortality, she had become not only their teacher and guardian, but also their mother in many ways, she explained.

"But why?" Lucy asked. "Why did you choose Aluna, Snow, Opal, and Scarlet to become VamPixies?"

"Although we appeared to be mere mortals, our mothers were not," Opal said proudly. "Our mothers had special abilities. They originated from Xiemoon, from a tribe of Xie women who were gifted at herbal magic."

"Then why did they live on The Outside?" Lucy asked.

Snow explained, "They left Xiemoon before we were born because they were imprisoned for practicing their craft. They were experts at herbal healing, had invented many life-saving medicines and saved many Xie lives. But there were some Xie folk who didn't like them, who claimed that they were evil witches who were poisoning people. One day, the Xie king passed a law that prohibited all women from practicing medicine or magic within the tribe. Only men were allowed to heal the sick."

"So when our mothers were caught making tonics and salves from herbs, they were jailed in a cave," Opal said. "But, the Xie leaders who put them there obviously didn't know what our mothers were capable of. Everything necessary to create a spell for escape was right there in that cave—hair of mice, lime scale, ebony stone, cricket wings, and lavender, which my mother always carried in her pocket."

"Smart, beautiful women are often underestimated," Scarlet said, as she flipped her hair.

"They didn't want to leave Xiemoon, but decided they must cross over to The Outside where they could have their freedom, find new lives as humans, and practice their craft as they liked," Aluna said. "But once they had left Xiemoon, they couldn't come back. On The Outside, they took herbs that made them human size, and made a pact to never return, leaving Xiemoon behind forever. Eventually, they parted and went to different parts of the world to start new lives. They fell in love, married our mortal fathers, and each of them became pregnant with girls."

"We were all born on the same day," Scarlet said.

Lucy asked. "Did you know that you were part pixie when you were mortal?"

"Each of our mothers told us their story on our 13th birthdays, a few months before we died. It was almost like they knew what was going to happen to us, and wanted to explain it before Salu made us immortal VamPixies," Opal answered.

Aluna, who had broken away to the kitchen, interrupted the conversation. "Lunch is ready!"

Salu joined Lucy and the VamPixies at the table. While they ate, Lucy contemplated her friend's complicated existence, as well as her own. How tragic their mortal endings must have been. She finally asked, "So will you tell me about your lives before Xiemoon?"

"Yes, of course we will," Snow said. She smiled at Lucy from across the table. "No more secrets."

Lucy coughed quietly, knowing that she was still keeping a rather large one.

Opal got up and walked over to the fireplace mantle. She scooped up an arm full of the black and white photographs from the shelf and brought them to the table. She gave one each to Scarlet, Snow, and Aluna, kept one, and laid the others out on the table.

Snow pointed to one of the photos and said, "This one was taken of the four of us right after we came to Xiemoon."

On closer inspection, Lucy noticed the little pink training wings peeking out from behind the tightly bound corsets, long skirts, and lacey collars that they wore. The photo was dated 1897 in the corner.

"We were VamPixies in training, just like you," Aluna said to Lucy. "We were only thirteen. Actually, we're still only 13."

"1897?" Lucy asked, looking at the date. "So if you were thirteen in 1897, that makes you?"

"One hundred and twenty six," Opal said. "I guess there is one good thing about being immortal; we will never show our age."

"Wow, that's old!" Lucy said.

Lucy could hear the sadness in the voices of her friends, as they brought forward their photo and introduced their mortal family to her. Now she understood why they didn't like to talk about it. It was obviously painful and they missed their mortal families just as much today as they ever had. But now they had a new family, brought together by death and strengthened by their friendship and love for each other. The VamPixies were a family now.

Lucy picked up another picture and pointed to each of the girls, who had obviously graduated from their training status because they had big lavender wings in this picture. Salu was in the photo too, along with another woman that Lucy immediately recognized. It looked like the same girl that she imagined to be floating in the clouds outside her classroom window so long ago. "Violet. That looks like Violet," Lucy thought out loud.

"Who is that?" Lucy asked. "She looks familiar."

"That's Charlotte," Salu answered, "Charlotte Whitfield."

Just then, it all made sense to Lucy. Violet was actually her Great Granny Charlotte as a young girl—the one who had come to her in a vision outside her classroom window. That's what started it all.

"Do you know her?" Snow asked.

"She's my great grandmother! Come on, you can't tell me that you didn't know that I was related to Charlotte Whitfield. It's just another one of your secrets!" Lucy's eyes welled up and her voice tightened. Again, she felt a wave of betrayal wash over her. The VamPixies had lied by omission.

Opal, Aluna, Scarlet, and Snow, all stared at her blankly.

Lucy looked at the photo in her hands. She felt as if she had just been socked in the stomach. They must have known all along that she was Charlotte's great granddaughter, and they hadn't told her because they wanted to get their Xietu back. That must be why they had invited her to Xiemoon in the first place, she decided.

Lucy got up from her chair and blurted out, "You don't care about being my friend! I'm here because I was "chosen", right?"

"You are Charlotte's lineage?" Snow grabbed a hold of the photograph that Lucy was clutching, but the silver frame slipped from between their hands and dropped onto the floor, shattering the glass that covered the antique photo.

"Let's not pretend any more," Lucy said. She turned away from the winged girls to look for Scratch. "I'm leaving!"

But before she could storm out, Salu placed her hand on Lucy's shoulder. "They aren't pretending. I knew Charlotte was your great grandmother, but they didn't. I didn't tell them that you are a Seer either. My girls were not aware that you are the one who I have been expecting all these years."

"Expecting?" Lucy asked bitterly.

Salu continued, "I'm so sorry to have hurt you, Lucy. I did not tell the girls that you were Charlotte's descendent because I wanted to be certain that you could handle your Mind Sight and the responsibility that may come with Charlotte's prophecy."

Opal said, "We promise Lucy, we didn't know. We honestly just wanted to have you as a friend."

"If you want to be angry at someone, be angry with me, not them," Salu said.

"Prophecy?" Snow asked. Clearly, she hadn't heard of this either.

"Charlotte was also a Seer, and she saw that one day in the future, Xiemoon would be threatened again by evil and her lineage—you—would come to help us. Her prophecy is coming true."

"Which means that we are in some sort of danger?" Aluna asked.

"Apparently so," Salu said.

Lucy stood still, unsure how to feel about what she had just learned. How could she be Xiemoon's savior? The girls all stared at her as if they didn't understand how this could be either. Lucy could see that they didn't know anything about her relation to Charlotte or Charlotte's prophecy.

"I'm sorry," Lucy said to them. She took a deep breath and released it. " And...I lost the Xietu."

"What did you say?" Salu asked. "Why do you think that you lost the Xietu?"

Lucy admitted, "Because I found it, and then I put it back, and now it's gone."

Salu said, "I thought that Charlotte wore the Xietu to her grave where it would be safe forever."

"No, she hid it in a cave back home. I found it, but I put it back because I thought it made Scratch sick. I didn't know what it was or that it was so important to you, until it was too late. When I went back to get it, I found Edge's necklace there," Lucy said as she reached into her pocket, pulled out the crystal pendant and showed it to the girls. "I know I messed up everything. I should just go back home."

"You should have told us. Our society is in serious danger if the Xietu is missing," Salu said. "But no, Lucy, we do not want you to go home. You are part of our family, no matter what you did."

"And we need you to help us save Xiemoon," Snow said to Lucy, as she, Scarlet, Aluna, and Opal encircled Lucy.

"But I don't understand how I can save Xiemoon. I'm just a regular mortal girl. You're the one with all the magic and wings and everything. Can't you just ask the moon where the Xietu is?"

"No, it doesn't work like that," Opal said. "The moon can help to guide us to what is right, but we cannot see the future as you can. The moon shows us who needs our healing on The Outside, but we don't have the Mind Sight. Only you do."

"Come on Lucy, I would kill to be a Seer like you," Scarlet said.

"But look," Lucy said, pointing to her little pink wings. "How can I help with these? I couldn't save anything."

Lucy walked away from the group, trying to hold her emotions in, but a few tears escaped. She felt useless and weak, standing at one of the tall castle windows, avoiding the gaze of the VamPixies who were expecting more from her than she felt she could give. Lucy strummed the clear glass lightly with her fingertips while she watched the mist roll away and reveal the lavender moon. She had forgotten that her Mind Sight could be triggered easily if she caught sight of the moon. Her knees buckled, but she steadied herself by leaning on the back of a nearby chair. "Uh oh, I'm getting light headed again!"

The VamPixies surrounded Lucy, watching as her green eyes glazed over and she dropped to the floor.

A vision of Edge standing in front of the Moonsprite's fortress came into Lucy's mind. He was smiling broadly as he swung the Xietu talisman in front of Zen's face. Next he landed in a thicket of trees and placed the talisman in the wrinkled palm of a woman who looked a lot like a creepy version of Salu, but with wiry dark hair and blood red wings.

The image disappeared from Lucy's mind as quickly as it came.

Salu rushed over to Lucy. "Oh dear girl, you must employ your will to steady yourself when The Mind Sight comes. We'll have to work on that. Are you all right?"

20

WHEN Lucy awoke from her vision of Edge and the Salu look-alike, she saw the real Salu kneeling over her and Opal, Scarlet, Snow and Aluna looking on.

"What did you see, Lucy?" Salu asked.

Still dazed, Lucy didn't answer. She was too busy thinking about what she had just seen. Salu was right there and her hair was still white, so who was the wild haired likeness she had just seen?

"Lucy, are you okay?" Salu asked.

But when she leaned in to touch Lucy's forehead, Lucy saw something even more unsettling. A heavy silver medallion swung out from under Salu's silk collar and dangled over her velvet robe. The very Xietu talisman that Lucy thought was lost had just been found, and it was hanging around Salu's neck.

Taken aback by this sighting, Lucy scuttled away from Salu's reach like a bug that was about to be squished, and jumped to her feet.

"How did you get that?" Lucy accused, pointing to the exposed Xietu.

Salu looked down at her chest. "Oh, this?" she asked as she cupped her hand over the shiny Xietu. "This one is mine. Charlotte wore the other. There are two matching talismans."

Lucy hung her head and took a seat in the parlor. "You scared me. I just had a vision of Edge giving the other one to a woman who looked just like you. Who is she? I could have sworn it was you, but she had black hair and red wings. She has the second talisman."

Salu's face went pale. "Her name is Salena...it must be recovered before it's too late."

"Too late for what?" Lucy asked.

"Lucy, let me explain. There is one final piece of information that I haven't told you," Salu confessed. "I have an identical sister named Salena. Like the Xietu, we are twins, but she has black hair and her wings are crimson."

"And she's evil," Opal added.

"Before he died, my father, Angus, discovered a very rare gemstone at Xienite Mountain. This is only half of the Seizerstone he found," Salu said, fingering the sparkling violet gem in the center of her talisman. "The whole Seizerstone gives the person who possesses it the ability to control the minds of others. The stone's keeper can become a Siezer and take possession of another's thoughts. This can be a dangerous power in the wrong hands. That's why my father split the gem in half, and set them into two talismans; one for me and the other one for my sister. He trusted us not to abuse the Seizerstone's power."

"So the Xietu that Charlotte left for me in the cave belonged to Salena?" Lucy asked.

"Yes," Salu said. "You see, Papa was never made immortal like us, and after he died, Salena changed. She was angry with him for refusing to be turned VamPixie and leaving us. Eventually, her bitterness turned to hate for everyone around her. That's when she began studying our father's spell manuscripts to increase her powers."

Aluna added, "Salena wanted to be like the vampires who bit her—if you know what I mean."

"I had no choice but to try and stop her from ruining the VamPixie way of life," Salu said. "Charlotte and I created an invisible prison to hold Salena safely at Xienite Mountain. We hoped that she would change her ways, but even after all these years, she still wants to hurt everyone she comes in contact with."

"That's terrible!" Lucy said.

"As long as Salena is not in possession of her Xietu, she can't get out of her mountain prison," Salu explained. "However, she is still a feared opponent. She is very clever, and if she ever gets a hold of her Xietu again, her magic will be just as strong as mine, and she will gain back her Formling abilities."

Before Lucy had a chance to ask what a Formling was, Salu stood up from her chair unexpectedly. Her whole body had begun to glisten, as if she had just been dusted with glitter. Then her form started to fade, and Lucy could see right through her—literally. The distinguished silver haired High Priestess of Xiemoon was no longer a VamPixie, but a swirling cloud of crystal dust. All that was left of Salu was her sparkles. Those disappeared too.

Lucy gasped when a green eyed silver fox emerged from behind the chair. Must be the new Salu, Lucy thought.

Scratch hopped up from his slumber and began to bark and whine at the other four-legged animal in the room. But the little fox ran behind the chair, and Salu's regal form reappeared, first as sparkly dust, and then as her solid-self.

"I am a Formling and so is my sister," Salu said. "The Xietu will allow her to take any form she wants."

"This is all my fault," Lucy said, as she looked into the eyes of each VamPixie in the room. "And I want to make it right, but I don't know how."

"I do," Scarlet said. "Let's go get the Xietu together!" And she put her arm around Lucy.

Aluna asked, "Do you think Edge has given it to Salena yet? Or was your Mind Sight a future vision."

"I don't know," Lucy said. She tried to recall exactly what she saw. "It went so fast. All I remember was that Edge was swinging the Xietu in front of Zen's face. There was fog around the Moonsprites fortress, but the moon was clear above it. Then Edge was in the bushes and I saw Salena appear from nowhere and take the talisman from him. That's it."

"Wait. Was the moon directly over the Moonsprite's fort?" Opal asked.

"Yeah, that's what it looked like."

"Well then it was probably about midnight when Edge was with Zen," Opal said. "You can tell time by the position of the moon you know." She looked to the grandfather clock, which had just chimed once at half past eight.

"If we hurry, we can stop Edge before he gives it to Salena," Snow said. "Let's go to the Moonsprite's fortress first. He'll probably still be there."

Scarlet, Aluna, Opal, and Snow all readied themselves to help Lucy win back the talisman. Lucy watched as they armed themselves with tiny vials of brightly colored liquids and herbs that they selected carefully from a cabinet in the parlor. She secretly worried that their potions wouldn't be enough to stop Edge this time.

"Let's have a toast for good luck," Salu said, and went off to the kitchen while the girls discussed their plans. She soon appeared with five tiny teacups and saucers on a tray. Lucy thought that they were almost the size of the toy ones that belonged to her little sister, Mara. The glass cups were full of a dark syrupy looking juice. It was the color of blood, and if Lucy didn't know better, she would have been alarmed.

"Mmmmm!" the VamPixies hummed. They seemed quite excited about the drink.

Salu put down the tray, and everyone gathered around her. Each VamPixie and Salu took a cup.

"What is it?" Lucy asked stiffly.

"Its sugar bean nectar," Salu said. "We have it on special occasions. Its delicious and good for your health."

"Oh, okay," Lucy said. She took the last cup and held it up for a toast with her friends.

"Here's to friendship, a safe journey, and the return of the Xietu," Salu said.

"Here's to Lucy!" Opal said as their crystal cups clinked together.

While the others took it all in one gulp, Lucy took a small sip to see if she liked it. The sugar bean nectar tasted sweet, yet spicy and warm as she swallowed. She too emptied the tiny cup.

Opal's cheeks were flushed and when she smiled, Lucy noticed that her teeth were stained pink and her fangs were extended. When Opal noticed that Lucy was looking at her, she closed her mouth and turned away. "Sorry Lucy, it's only temporary."

A few seconds later, Opal's fangs had retracted, but her skin had turned pinker than its normal pale tone. As if someone had flipped her light switch on, Opal was illuminated once again. In fact, all the girls were beginning to glow. Lucy felt a surge of electricity running through her body.

Salu handed each girl two large square lumps of sugar bean crystals. "You may need to replenish your strength later. Your glow will give you the extra strength you need against Salena."

"We VamPixies can't go without sufficient intake of sugar bean. We have low blood sugar," Snow said with a smile.

"Careful Lucy," Opal said, pointing to the empty cup in her hands. It had cracked under her newfound strength.

"Oh gosh, I didn't mean to do that," Lucy said. She placed the cup as gently as she could on the tray that Salu was holding. "This is so cool!"

"Are you ready?" Salu asked Lucy, and the other glowing, glittery girls behind her.

"Yes!" they all replied in unison, and headed for the door.

Scratch, who had been sleeping on a pillow next to the fire, barked to Lucy, and sauntered over to her feet. "No Scratch. You can't come this time. I want you to stay here in the castle where you'll be safe." Scratch must have understood, because he sighed and went back to his bed.

Outside, the glowing collective held hands tightly around Salu, who led them in the VamPixie Promise, the full moon shining brightly above them. Just as the VamPixies and Lucy finished the last verse, Lucy doubled over in pain.

"Ouch! My back hurts. It feels like my bones are splitting!" Lucy cried. She hunched over. Her trusted training wings began flapping wildly, detached their stringy suctions from her back, and fluttered toward the moon like a little pink moth to the light. And from the empty space along her spine, small spikes began to emerge, lifting and stretching her skin.

"What is happening?" Lucy screamed and dropped to her knees. She couldn't breathe and her heart was racing.

The girls and Salu encircled her. They joined hands, creating a blue field of electricity around her, which helped to numb the sharp pain she felt as the tips of her wings ripped through her skin and clothes to free themselves from the confines they had been trapped in.

It had finally happened. Lucy's real, amethyst encrusted VamPixie wings erupted from the place they had always been. Lucy had become a fully-fledged, Honorary VamPixie, wings and all.

Like a newly hatched sparrow, the baby bird stretched one wing straight and then the other. Lucy felt triumphant as her wings glistened under the moonlight. The magical blue aura around her faded away.

Salu ran her healing "V" lightly around the wounds that were caused by her wing's arrival. To Lucy's surprise, she could feel it when Salu touched the tips and when the wind blew softly over their slick surface. These beautiful appendages were as much a part of her body as her gangly arms and legs.

"I guess I was ready," Lucy whispered as she felt herself intensely alive for the first time ever. Her entire body tingled with strength and power, wings included. Her mind was certain that life at that moment was as it should be. Right then, Lucy felt her destiny.

"Yes," Salu said proudly, "You were ready. When you come back with the Xietu, we will celebrate the coming of your wings."

This time, Lucy led the VamPixies in flight. It felt as natural as breathing, and more wonderful than anything she had experienced—ever. Soaring above the glittering landscape, she illuminated the sky around her. Scarlet, Snow, Aluna, and Opal, trailed in her light. They were five glowing stars streaking through the indigo sky, toward the Moonsprites' fortress, to claim what was theirs before it was too late. The fate of Xiemoon was in their hands.

But as Lucy was nearing the edge of the thick forest, which surrounded the barren dragon pit, she noticed several dark-winged silhouettes hovering above their destination.

Circling the dark, spiky roofline of the Moonsprite stronghold, were six deep violet winged creatures. They appeared to be VamPixies of sorts, Lucy thought, but they did not glow or sparkle. No, they had no visible light at all. If it wasn't for their pale blue skin, Lucy may not have seen them.

"Wait!" Lucy threw her glowing arms out wide and stopped, hovering in the mist. Snow, Opal, Scarlet, and Aluna soon arrived her side.

"What are those?" Lucy asked.

"Those are Shadow Girls," Aluna said.

"Are they friendly?" Lucy asked.

"Definitely not," Opal said.

21

Lucy squinted to see the pack of shadowy wings that were flying under the moon in front of her, but they had faded into the darkness, and the moon was no longer a perfect sphere, but had become a blurry ball. The same burning pressure that she had felt in her eyes the last time her Mind Sight paid a visit, had returned.

"Not again, not here," Lucy said to herself.

The extra-strength she had acquired from her Glow felt like it had been drained right out of her. Lucy's entire body went soft. Even her powerful new wings felt as if they had turned into butter that had just melted onto warm toast. Lucy screamed and flailed her limp limbs through the thick air, but her body and wings would only move in slow motion. Her free-fall toward the hard ground below had begun.

Lucy could not see the ground coming closer because her Mind Sight had taken over and flooded her brain with an image of Edge, who was walking through a grove of trees, smiling and swinging the Xietu like a lasso over his head. A grey-skinned arm reached out for him, but this was all Lucy saw before Aluna and Opal swooped in and grabbed her by the tips of her wings, just before she landed face first into the bushes beneath her.

"Lucy, are you all right?" Opal asked.

"I think so," she answered softly.

Snow and Scarlet took Lucy's hands, while Opal and Aluna pulled her up by her wings.

"Ouch! Be careful! They're still a little tender," Lucy said, referring to her newly hatched wings.

Snow ran her healing fingers down Lucy's cheek, across her forehead, and down her arm. Lucy wasn't sure what she was doing, but the soreness she felt from her fall went away immediately.

Lucy's heart raced as she caught her breath and reported on her brief vision. "Edge was in the woods. He had the Xietu, and then I saw a creepy looking arm, which I'm pretty sure belonged to Salena. I think Edge is already with her. I think we're too late."

"Maybe we should go to Xienite Mountain instead," Opal said, looking toward the dark winged silhouettes that hovered over the fortress in the distance.

Scarlet added, "Then we can skip fighting the Shadow Girls for the Xietu. I'm sure that's why they're here too."

"They do look kind of bad—tough, I mean," Lucy said. "And I…"

"Oh no, her eyes are sparkling again. Lucy!" Aluna said, and reached out to steady her friend.

Lucy leaned against Aluna's shoulder while Snow grabbed her other arm, and Scarlet and Opal held her droopy wings. Lucy could feel that they were transmitting some of their energy to her. She did not collapse this time. With their help, and all the strength she could muster in her Jell-O legs, she remained standing strong, as her Mind Sight took over once again.

Great Granny Charlotte's youthful face smiled at Lucy. Her hair was chocolate and wavy, and her milky skin was sprinkled with pink freckles. Charlotte said, "Help the Shadow Girls. They will help you too."

Lucy reached out, hoping to touch her great grandmother's lovely face, but it was not Charlotte that she touched. It was Snow, who stood in front of her. "What did you see, Lucy?" she asked.

"Charlotte. We're supposed to help the Shadow Girls," Lucy murmured weakly and shrugged her shoulders. "But, I think I need to rest first."

Aluna said, "We need to balance her energy, or she isn't going to be strong enough to go on."

Snow, Opal, Scarlet, and Aluna made a circle around Lucy and placed their hands on each other's shoulders. Aluna said, "You must learn to balance the earth and moon energy. The earth will ground you and give you physical strength, while the moon gives you knowledge and access to your Mind Sight. Your earth energy is very weak right now."

Lucy nodded in agreement and looked to the small circle of earth that sparkled beneath her feet.

"Now close your eyes," Aluna instructed.

Aluna continued whispering in what Lucy thought to be Visphixie—because she couldn't understand a word of it. She didn't see what was happening around her, but she felt it. It started as a tickle in the soles of her feet, as if there were roots growing out of them, snaking down into the earth. And then she felt the roots begin to warm, and an electric type of heat traveled back up through her body to the very top of her head. The muscles in her shaky limbs tightened, as the earth's energy pumped through her. Lucy's wings fluttered gently, as if they were telling her that they were ready to fly again.

Aluna stopped whispering. Lucy heard nothing, except for a light wind passing over her ears. "You can open your eyes now," she said softly. "But don't move."

Lucy was covered by what looked to her like crystallized light vines. The transparent vessels had sprouted up from the earth around her feet, and grown her head. She was enclosed in a web of earthly energy. She smiled and soaked it in.

A moment later, Aluna waved her arms over her head, and the vines disappeared back into the earth from which they came.

"Thanks, I feel stronger now," Lucy said.

"When you feel weak, you must connect with the earth," Aluna said. "We follow the moon, but we also need strength from the earth."

Just then, a high-pitched scream came from the direction of the Moonsprite's fortress.

"I'm ready," Lucy said. "Let's go talk to the Shadow Girls."

Scarlet stepped forward. "What? No way! Those Shadow Girls hate us and they'll just hide anyway. They could attack us and we wouldn't even see them coming."

"Are you afraid of them?" Lucy asked.

"Me? No!" Scarlet said. "I just don't like them."

"Oh, because if you're afraid, you can stay here and wait for us," Lucy said.

Scarlet folded her arms over her chest and scowled at Lucy.

Opal said, "One time, Ivy came out of nowhere and pushed Scarlet into the sugar bean tree, and her wing was punctured by a branch. There was blood everywhere! She could have died!"

Lucy thought that Opal was just being dramatic. "How could she have died from a punctured wing? I thought vampires had to get a stake through their heart to die?"

"We are VamPixies, not vampires," Scarlet said, giving Lucy a look of disgust. "Our wings are the only part of us that is alive. If our wings bleed, we can die if they aren't healed. Our wings are as vital to us as a heart is to a mortal being."

Lucy said, "Oh, I didn't know."

"I'm afraid that I might want to retaliate if I see Ivy again," Scarlet said. "And I might not be able to control myself."

"Maybe we should just go find Edge and Salena," Aluna said. "The Shadow Girls are only going to cause trouble for us."

"I think we need to listen to Lucy," Snow said. "She is the one with the Mind Sight."

"Charlotte told me that the Shadow Girls would help us. I have to trust my Mind Sight."

"Whatever," Scarlet said.

"We all need to work together to get the Xietu back," Lucy said. "Remember the VamPixie code? It's about time you made peace with your enemies. We are all VamPixies, right?"

Scarlet looked down at the ground and turned away from the group. She paused for a moment, took a deep breath, and asked, "Who's going first?"

"I will," Lucy said.

After eating one of the sugar bean candies that Salu had given them, the VamPixies, Lucy included, decided to face the Shadow Girls. Their glowing forms ascended into the dark indigo sky.

The violet shadows that had been circling the Moonsprite's fortress disappeared almost immediately from view. "They must have seen us. They're hiding!" Scarlet yelled.

Lucy looked down to the glistening crystal landscape below. She was thankful that the dragon pit was empty on this night. This was one less thing to worry about.

"Oh no!" Snow screamed.

From nowhere and everywhere the dragons appeared, breathing fire and screeching with primeval terror as they flew towards the VamPixies. The dragons that were built with metal and held together with rusted nuts and bolts were no longer earthbound, but powered by roaring engines that pushed steam towards the earth below! The Moonsprites had definitely made improvements on the creatures since their last grounded attack. Not only were they airborne, but they moved with the agility of a real living thing.

Lucy turned just in time to meet the glistening crystal eyes of one dragon that had screamed in from behind them. The dragon opened its silver fanged jaws and burst fire from its tubular throat. But Lucy zipped out of the way, narrowly dodging the flames. While that one flew past and turned around, another one came from the opposite direction. This one was faster, and Lucy only managed to swoop down beneath its rusted belly seconds before it snapped its jaws closed on the air, inches from the tip of her wing.

Lucy fled the open dragon pit for the forest of trees that surrounded it, hoping to hide, but she had forgotten that her entire body was glowing, which made hiding impossible, even under the thick greenery that covered her. Soon, the rumble of steam that powered one dragon was directly above Lucy. Branches scratched against her wings as she flew through the trees, and the rust bucket above her hurled flames, lighting the forest on fire and forcing Lucy deeper into the bush.

"Ouch!" she screamed, as she felt a branch slice her arm, and a cluster of vines wrap around her wing as if it had just reached out and grabbed her. Lucy struggled against the tree, ripping the vines away easier than she expected she could; until that moment, she had forgotten about her extra strength. Lucy grabbed a branch from the tree and threw it at the metal dragon, hitting it squarely in the head. The dragon's head flew off its writhing neck, and tumbled to the ground. The body followed, exploding into a cloud of steam and dust as it hit the ground. One down!

The forest was in flames. Lucy couldn't see her friends through the thickening smoke. She buried her nose and mouth in the crook of her elbow, hoping it would help her breathe, but she was forced to drop to the ground to escape it.

She called out, "Where are you?" All she could see was smoke and aside from racing engines, she couldn't hear a thing. After catching her breath, Lucy bounded back up through the smoky cloud layer to find clearer skies.

Her cries had been heard, not by the VamPixies, but by two dragons that had just emerged from the fiery forest. Again Lucy hid her face in the crook of her elbow and dropped back under the smoke-filled tree line, hoping to find another weapon to use against the giant machines. This could take one of them down, she thought as she bent down over a very large rock. Employing all her strength, Lucy picked up the rock, took a deep breath, and thrust herself up through the haze. As she rose above it, she realized that she was trapped; one dragon was on her left and one was on her right. Lucy screamed as she chucked the rock as hard as she could at the one on her right side. She missed.

And now the machines looked frighteningly mad, as if they were angry with Lucy and wanted revenge. She wondered how the Moonsprite boys could be controlling these beasts when they were nowhere to be seen? Did they have remote control computers? Lucy was becoming more and more convinced that these dragons were acting alone. They were powered by mechanics, but there was definitely something in their red crystal eyes that made them look alive.

With nowhere else to go, Lucy pulled her wings to her body and plummeted to the earth below as each dragon shot orange flames toward her. From below, she heard them scream at her absence.

"Blow them down!" shouted a voice.

"What?" Lucy yelled, not understanding what she was supposed to do, or from where the voice was coming.

Again, she heard, "Blow them down!" Lucy recognized Snow's voice.

As she scanned the sky to find her friends, Scarlet's swooped in and grabbed her hand, pulling her up above the smoky air to join the others, forming a line across the sky. The VamPixies took in a deep breath and proceeded to blow a hurricane strength wind at the two remaining dragons.

It looked as if the dragons were flying in slow motion, barely moving forward against the gale winds created by the VamPixies. The dragon's only defense was fire, which was blown back into them, igniting their writhing heads and bodies. Lucy fanned her wings at hyper-speed, adding to the force that was stopping these formidable machines.

From inside their bodies, sparks fizzled and popped. Within seconds, their engines shut down, their heads imploded, and they crashed to the earth. A fiery blaze erupted as each dragon hit the ground.

Snow shouted to the others, "We have to stop the forest fire from spreading! We must invoke our rain spell!"

"How do we do that?" Lucy asked.

"Just follow our lead, and visualize rain with us, okay?"

Lucy nodded yes and took the hands of Opal and Snow, who had formed a circle with Scarlet and Aluna. Lucy closed her eyes and thought about how it would feel to have rain-drops on her shoulders, and then how it would feel for rain to soak her hair, her body, and her wings. As she imagined this happening, the circle of friends began to spin. Lucy felt like she was on a merry-go-round. Then the ride got faster and faster, until Lucy's grip was slipping off of Opal and Snow's wrists. As her fingers let go, and she tumbled in slow motion towards the earth, she heard her friends scream in unison, "Xiekallory!"

All five VamPixies had descended to the crystal dragon pit. Lucy sat on the ground and started to laugh at what had just happened. It was kind of fun.

Snow stood up and held her palms up to the sky. First one drop fell, then another and then it began to pour. It rained so hard that within minutes, the forest fire was out, the smoke had been washed from the sky, and all that was left of the burning dragon heap was a steamy pile of blackened metal parts. Several red crystals that had once been their eyes were still glowing vibrantly next to the wreckage.

The wet VamPixies walked closer, and Lucy bent down to inspect the gems. "What are these?" Lucy asked.

"They look like Life Essence Crystals from Xienite Mountain," Snow said. "Finders keepers." She tucked them into the leather pouch that hung over her shoulder.

Other than the moon and stars, the sky was empty now and it was completely silent. The evil dragon beasts had been eliminated, but where had the Shadow Girls gone? Lucy fluttered her wings and motioned to the others to follow her back up into the sky.

"Come on out, Shadow Girls!" Lucy yelled, hoping to get their attention.

There was no reply.

"Maybe they ran home," Scarlet said. "They must be afraid of us!" she yelled.

"We are not afraid of VamPixies!" a voice shouted back from a small outcropping of rocks on the desert floor.

"Shhh!" another voice said from the same area.

"The voices…they're coming from down there," Lucy said, pointing down to the empty rocks. "Let's go have a look." They floated down, landing on top of a sparkling boulder—a real one this time.

"Look there," Opal whispered, pointing to a wet wing tip that stuck out from under the rock. "That's a Shadow Girl's wing."

The VamPixies jumped down and cautiously peered under the cave-like formation to find a lone, wounded Shadow Girl. She was shivering and lying on her side with her dark purple wings draped over her, which had been blackened and burned raw in spots. There was a pool of wet blood that had spilled from a gash that spanned the length of her right wing. She lifted her head and glared at the VamPixies.

"Go away!" the Shadow Girl screamed. She must have been in great pain, because tears had cleaned a path down her dirty cheeks.

"Ivy, you are hurt," Snow said. "You need help."

"No! Go away," Ivy threatened. "Leave me be! Do not touch me!"

"Okay," Scarlet said. As she attempted to walk away, Snow stopped her.

Lucy turned to her friends and whispered, "We have to help her."

Snow inched toward the wounded girl, "We will heal you...if you let us."

"I said no!" Ivy screamed, and sat up on the muddy earth. She pulled her black velvet hood over her head to shield her face from her glowing enemies. "I do not want your sparkles."

Lucy whispered to Opal, "What is she talking about?"

"If we heal her, her wings will become like ours," Opal explained quietly. "Pretty."

Scarlet knelt down and peeked under the hood of Ivy's jacket. "Then I guess we'll just leave you under your rock to die." She stood up and walked away. Scarlet's face was serious and about as red as her hair.

"Please just let us help you," Lucy said to Ivy. "Then we'll leave you alone."

"No!"

"But, we need your help," Lucy said. "We need a new leader."

"What?" Scarlet protested, coming back to the group.

Lucy mouthed the words, "Trust me," to her friends and then continued trying to convince Ivy to let them heal her.

"Well, we were wondering if you would lead us to Xienite Mountain to find Edge," Lucy said. "He went there to free Salena from her prison and give her the Xietu. If she possesses the talisman, she will get her power back. We can't let that happen. We need your help."

Ivy sneered, "Why should I help you pathetic pastel girls get the Xietu? I'm a little tired of you VamPixies always being in charge. What's in it for us?"

Snow said, "Your safety—that's what's in it for you. Salena threatens to turn Xiemoon into a bloodthirsty society again, endangering both VamPixies and Shadow Girls. We need to get the Xietu back to Salu, so that Salena stays locked up where she belongs."

"Wait a minute. How do you know that Edge is going to give the Xietu to Salena?" Ivy asked. "Maybe he wants to keep it for himself."

"Because she is Charlotte Whitfield's lineage," Opal said, pointing at Lucy. "She saw it. She has the Mind Sight, just like Charlotte did."

Lucy didn't know why, but this little bit of knowledge seemed to change Ivy's attitude immediately. Ivy stared hard at Lucy, looking her up and down for several minutes.

"Charlotte was once a good friend to me," Ivy said, her eyes penetrating Lucy's. "I'll do it for Charlotte."

Nothing else needed to be said.

Encircling the reluctant Shadow Girl, the VamPixie tribe held up their peace fingers and spread their healing light over Ivy's wings. Burned and raw, her skins slowly turned back to the shadowy slick purple that they had been. She sighed with relief as the burning pain cooled and the pink electric aura surrounding her faded away. Then Ivy's transformation began. From dark violet, to dusky purple, to a lovely light amethyst, her wings sparkled with moonlit jewels.

Ivy looked at her twinkling wings with disgust and let out a high-pitched whistle.

Six Shadow Girls emerged from the crystal earth of the dragon pit to meet their newly glittered leader. Lucy guessed that they had been right there, all along, camouflaged as earth or rock, or whatever they were hiding as before they appeared dressed in the dark shades of night.

They snickered at Ivy's beautified wings. When she glared back at them, they took on a more somber expression. Ivy introduced her reluctant tribe to the one they were about to join forces with.

"This is Samaire, Vivian, Nora, Sage, Josephine, and Amelia. Together," Ivy said, "we will protect Xiemoon!"

"We better hurry," Lucy added. "I have a bad feeling that we might be too late."

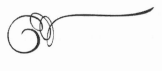

* *

22

Salena

"**Finally,** Papa, I have my power back," Salena whispered to the tiny field mouse that sat silently in the palm of her hand. Her spindly grey fingers stroked the mouse's fur as she turned her back to Edge. "Don't tell him, but I lied!" Salena snickered. "Now that I have the Xietu, there's no need for him. He'll never be King of Xiemoon. Stupid boy. I'll get rid of him soon, and you and I will rule together."

"Salena, my Queen, are we going to VamPixie castle now?" Edge called from several yards away.

"Don't bother me," Salena ordered. She walked even further away, ignoring his presence.

"I'll teach them a lesson," she said to the mouse, "and then they'll understand that I am not the crazy one, Salu is. Right? Yes, I agree with you Papa, she must be stopped! We VamPixies are vampires, after all, and the thirst for blood is boiling in us!" Salena slid her tongue along the sharp ends of her fangs. "My sister will not deny Xiemoon's immortals of their right to bite."

Salena shoved the mouse into her pocket, clutched the silver talisman that dangled over her heart, and stopped at the edge of the invisible wall of energy, which had contained her for over one hundred years. She felt the anger of an entire century boiling in her veins. Salena's nostrils flared and she growled with hatred as she though of the ones who had jailed her.

She turned to Edge, who had come closer, and said, "My time has come! Now I can break the spell, and rule Xiemoon...with you as King and me as Queen, of course."

Edge smiled at Salena.

"Just remember, I gave you those fangs," Salena said. "And I can take them away."

What she really wanted to do was sink her teeth into his scrawny little neck at that very moment and quench her bloodlust. No, she couldn't, not until she had both Xietu talismans in her possession. Besides, she might need him later.

Right now, the time had come to fly out of the invisible walls that had imprisoned her at Xienite Mountain. Salu and Charlotte had taken away her freedom by building an energy field around her that she could not escape from. Others could come in, but she could not leave. Salena kissed the shining stone in the talisman's center and thought how it might feel when she would have both halves talismans. Her revenge would be satisfied when she dominated Xiemoon as a Siezer. What fun she would have then!

"Follow me Boy," she said.

Standing at the edge of her invisible cage with the Xietu hanging around her neck, Salena lifted her shiny crimson wings in preparation to fly for the first time in over a century. The moon above her had hidden behind a wall of clouds. She closed her eyes and took her last breath in captivity.

With hatred erupting from her soul, Salena unleashed a primal scream and sprung into the air. The invisible prison walls shattered like glass and disintegrated into dust. Salina's blood red wings carried her out of the dark thicket, up to a crystal covered plateau at the very top of Xienite Mountain.

Edge touched down next to her.

This was the beginning of the ruthless revenge that she planned to inflict on Salu and Charlotte. Well, Charlotte was already dead, she reminded herself, but there was Lucy wasn't—yet. "I can't wait to meet her," Salena said to herself.

"I smell VamPixies!" Salena giggled and ran her pointed tongue along the edges of her yellowed fangs. "When will they be here?"

"Let's see," Edge said, digging into his pocket. He pulled out a small shiny machine, slid open its cover, touched it a few times and then stared at it. "Zen says that they are on their way."

"What's that thing?" Salena asked him.

"It's a machine that we use to communicate. We got it from The Outside." He said.

The giant pillars that bordered the Xienite Mountain's high plain sparkled around Salena and Edge as they waited in quiet anticipation. Salena remembered this to be the very spot where she and her sister Salu received the twin Xietu talismans from her father before he died. She smiled when she thought of how her father fit the Xietu halves together and turned them gently to form one, causing the Seizerstone to alight. His words echoed in Salena's mind, "Rule Xiemoon together—peacefully as one." Then he split the Xietu and gave half to each of them.

But Salena's memory faded quickly, as she heard a voice in her head say, "Salu is evil. You must rule alone."

Salena wrenched her bony fingers around Edge's wrist. "Yes, Papa, I will destroy her!"

"What? Why are you calling me Papa?" Edge asked.

She didn't answer, but let go of Edge's arm immediately, and stroked her cold fingers across the warm little mouse in her pocket.

"So why are we waiting for the VamPixies?" Edge asked. "I thought we were going to steal the other talisman from Salu. She's at VamPixie Castle. We need that to complete our plan. Don't we?"

"We do need it, but before we pay my sister a visit, we need to do something else. We need to kill Charlotte's lineage," she answered.

"WE?" he asked. "Why do WE have to kill her?"

"Revenge, stupid," she hissed, "and once she's dead, it'll be even easier to take the Xietu from the VamPixies. They won't break that stupid Promise."

"You told me that YOU were going to do it," Edge said. "I was just supposed to bring you the Xietu."

"Is the little man scared to kill?" Salena asked, moving close and looking down at the boy who was much shorter than she. "What are those fangs for if you're not going to use them?"

"I'm not afraid to use them!" Edge insisted.

"Good," Salena said, and stroked Edge's coppery mop of hair. "Then after we've drained her blood, we'll stake the wings of the others and let them bleed to their immortal deaths." She considered her options for a moment as she tapped her pointed nails against her cheek. "I've changed my mind. I want to watch them become true vampires again. Besides, they're already dead. I want Salu to watch her precious prodigies become what they were meant to be—blood feeders."

"Oh, I get it," Edge said, "but if you kill Lucy, then Salu will make her a permanent VamPixie," he pointed out.

"Even better!" Salena said. She plucked the shivering mouse from her pocket and held it close to her wrinkled cheek. "Then she can become a blood feeder too. And I'll put them all in prison, and unleash them on The Outside to feed each night."

Edge smiled. "Hey, I know just how to sweeten Lucy's pain—Jax. She would do ANYTHING for Jax. We could kidnap him, bring him to Xiemoon, and hold him hostage in exchange for the other twin talisman."

Salena screamed, "Brilliant! Mouse, you are so clever." She kissed his little pink nose.

"But, I..."

"Quiet!" Salena shouted, and turned her back to Edge again.

Staring into the purple moon, still covered in clouds, Salena imagined Snow's face, her lavender wings, her youthful appearance. Salena's leathery skin and unkempt hair began to sparkle as her form became dust, swirling around and settling into the vision of Snow that she had just imagined. When the dust settled, Snow appeared, smiling sweetly.

Edge's jaw dropped. "You didn't tell me you were a Formling."

"I don't tell you everything. I'll be right back," Snow-Salena said in Snow's cheerful voice and sped off into the stars, leaving Edge all alone on top of Xienite Mountain.

Snow-Salena heard Edge call after her. "What am I supposed to do now?" he yelled.

But she didn't care to reply. She was on her way to The Outside to capture Jax. Because she had her Xietu, she had the power to go anywhere at the speed of light, and she could open the secret door without a key. Because she had just taken Snow's form, she had also attained Snow's knowledge. This allowed her to know how Jax smelled. She sniffed her way to where he lived, and seconds later, Snow-Salena squeezed through an opened window and landed in his bedroom.

"Jax, wake up!" Snow-Salena said as softly as she thought the real Snow would have said it. For effect, the now miniature VamPixie giggled and tickled his arm to wake him as she hovered over his bed. "Lucy needs your help!"

Jax fluttered his eyes and sat up in his bed. "What are you?" he asked the tiny girl.

"I'm a VamPixie. My name is Snow," Snow-Salena said as sweetly as possible.

"So you are for real?" Jax whispered.

Snow-Salena smiled, flipped her hair, and said, "I need your help, Jax! It's Lucy. She's been captured by Edge, and we need your help to free her."

"Okay, I'm coming," Jax said. He jumped out of bed and threw on his sneakers and a sweatshirt. "I'm ready."

Jax sprinted behind Snow-Salena through the woods toward the invisible door to Xiemoon. "Follow me," she said, and flew under the archway of red roses and vines.

Jax did as he was told and stepped through the passage. He stopped under the giant trees at the edge of this new world. "Hello! Snow? Where are we?"

Snow-Salena closed the door behind Jax and said, "Xiemoon."

Jax turned around. "Whoa! What happened to you?" He backed away from the VamPixie who was now a life-sized version of her miniature self.

Big Snow-Salena stared into his eyes. "So sorry to have startled you," she said with syrup on top. "We must hurry... for Lucy," she continued staring into his eyes, enchanting him into submission. "Hold my hand, and we'll get there faster."

"Yes, let's go." Jax took hold of her ice-cold hand and let Snow-Salena lead him to the edge of the rocky cliff that overlooked Xiemoon's wildflower valley. She jerked him into the air and laughed as he dangled helplessly, blowing about like a kite in the wind. In a matter of seconds, they landed on the top of Xienite Mountain.

Snow-Salena threw Jax to the ground. "Our bait has arrived!"

"So nice to see you again, Jax," Edge said.

"What the heck is going on here?" Jax asked. He picked himself up off the ground. "Who are you?"

Edge smiled and showed Jax his fangs. "Edge, future King of Xiemoon."

"Snow? Where did she go?" Jax asked.

But Snow-Salena had already begun her transformation back into glittering dust. She slowly revealed her shabby black clothes, wiry dark hair, and slick crimson wings to the boy she had so easily deceived.

Salena said, "You called?"

"Who are you?" Jax asked as he struggled to yank his arm out of her bony grip.

"I'm Salena, Salu's long lost sister, the one she locked up in this mountain prison for the past century."

"Where's Lucy?" Jax asked.

"Aw, so sweet!" Salena teased. "Don't fret, Boy. She'll be here momentarily," Salena laughed deeply at Jax's concern. "I just love to see people suffer."

"Oh look, here they come now," Edge said as he clapped and smiled, and pointed to the five glowing VamPixie stars above them. "Here we are! Down here!" Edge jumped up and down and waved at them.

"No, Lucy!" Jax yelled. "Stay away!"

Salena took the field mouse from her pocket, and held him up in her palm to see their visitor's arrival. "Look Papa, she's come. She's finally come!"

23

FROM Lucy's view, above the jagged crystal peak of Xienite Mountain, she could see that there were three people awaiting them. She expected two—Edge and Salena, but not three. Lucy swooped in closer to see who that third person was.

It was Jax. That changed everything.

She heard Jax warning her not to come, but there was no way that she would abandon her friend this time. Lucy signaled to Snow, Scarlet, Aluna, and Opal to land. The Shadow Girls had already camouflaged themselves somewhere into this new environment. The VamPixies circled the mountain peak and swooped in, surrounding Salena, Jax, and Edge.

Salena grabbed Jax from behind, and wrapped her creepy fingers around his forehead and neck, lifting him off the ground. Jax kicked and struggled to get loose for a few seconds and then went limp like a rag doll in her arms.

Lucy screamed, "Let him go!" At that moment, her anger exploded, and she lunged her glowing body at Salena with the intention of hurting her—badly. As Lucy hurled her body through the air, positioned to karate kick Salena, Edge took a shiny silver gadget from his pocket and shot a green laser beam at Lucy. Her attack came to a dead stop, and it wasn't because she suddenly remembered her VamPixie peace oath. This beam of fluorescent light penetrated her entire body, causing her to become covered in a cold green coating. Frozen solid, Lucy dropped to the ground like a heavy stone. When she hit, her icy covering broke into a million pieces.

With the wind knocked out of her, Lucy lay on the ground in a heap and watched Edge's boots skip closer to her body.

"Sorry, Lucy," Edge said. "I didn't mean to hurt you, but I thought you needed a gentle reminder that as a VamPixie, you absolutely cannot break the rules. No violence! I know you girls are all about the code."

"Thank you," Salena said to Edge. "Such a nice boy you are to remind her of her commitment to peace."

Lucy snarled at both of them and slowly brought her aching body to a standing position.

Salena mocked Lucy with an obviously fake, sweet giggle and then opened her mouth wide in a threatening smile. She pushed Jax's unconscious head to the side, exposed his neck, and glared at Lucy under her brow.

"No!" Lucy screamed.

But then Salena chuckled at her own sick sense of humor. "Don't worry, I won't kill him...yet." She squeezed Jax in her one-armed vice grip and kissed his cheek gently.

Snow, Opal, and Scarlet were now standing just a few feet away from Salena, and Aluna stood right beside Edge. Lucy waited for them to do something, anything to stop Salena from hurting Jax. Instead, they just stood there with wide-eyed blank faces, and made no moves whatsoever to help her. It was like they were in a trance. Edge too.

"Thank you for rescuing us!" Salena said, obviously trying to mimic her kind twin sister's voice. "I need your help. I want to make amends with my sister."

"I don't think so," Lucy said, not believing a word of it. "I'm not that stupid."

"No, you are very smart, just like your great grandmother. She was such a wonderful person," Salena said in an overly nice way. "I really do miss her."

"Liar!" Lucy said and glanced around again for help. The VamPixies still hadn't moved. The looked like useless zombies.

"I'll prove it to you." And then Salena laid Jax down gently at her feet and removed the Xietu talisman from her neck. She held it out to Lucy, as if she wanted to give it to her right then and there. Lucy watched the brightly shining Seizerstone, dangling a few mere steps away.

"Go ahead. Take it. It's yours. Charlotte wanted you to have this," Salena said.

That's when Lucy made a big mistake; She looked into Salena's scary pale blue eyes and was instantly drawn in—captured. She struggled against Salena's will, but she wasn't strong enough. She felt as if she were stuck in a nightmare where she couldn't run or scream to save herself.

"Didn't they tell you?" Salena asked. "That Charlotte and I were best friends... until my sister became jealous and turned her against me. It's all lies, Lucy. You shouldn't believe anything they say. In fact, I bet they didn't tell you that once you give them the Xietu, they're going to get rid of you. After they get what they want, they won't need you anymore," Salena warned.

"That's not true," Lucy said inside her mind. "We'll be friends forever."

"Oh yes, 'sisters of the night.' They're just playing with you," Salena continued, "using you to steal their precious Xietu, and once they're done with you, your memory will be erased and they will send you back to Crystal Creek wingless and powerless."

Salena's thoughts were invading and trying to replace her own, but what was left of Lucy's mind was still fighting. She knew that she needed some earthly energy to give her the strength she needed to resist Salena. So with all her might, Lucy concentrated on her feet and slowly began to pull the earth's energy up through her body, all the way to the top of her head. Her strength had returned.

"You know, there is only one way to become a real VamPixie, and that's to become immortal. That way, you can live here forever. No more Honorary VamPixie. You would like that, wouldn't you?" Salena asked. "Go ahead, you can speak now."

"No. I mean, yes, I would like that," Lucy said blankly, hoping that Salena wouldn't notice that she had broken free of her control. "What about Jax?"

"He can be immortal too," Salena replied.

Jax lifted his head from the ground and said, "Yeah Lucy, let's stay here in Xiemoon—together forever."

"I can help you to die," Salena whispered, reaching out to take Lucy's hand.

Although Lucy knew that although she had considered this option before, the cost was far too high. She didn't want to die, but had to agree with Salena. "Thank you," Lucy said.

Lucy reached her hand out as if she were going to take Salena's hand, but instead, grabbed at the Xietu! Salena jerked the Xietu away and clamped her bony hand around Lucy's arm. Lucy used her restored strength to break away and unleash a deafening scream that finally broke the hypnotic state that had held the VamPixies, Jax, the Shadow Girls, and even Edge at bay.

Seven Shadow Girls emerged from the crystal rocks that they had been camouflaged into, and jettisoned themselves toward Salena, descending over her in a mass of violet wings. Total chaos broke out on top of Xienite Mountain.

Lucy helped Jax to safety behind a crystal pillar. "Are you all right?"

"Yeah, I'm okay. Thanks," Jax said.

Salena swatted away the Shadow Girls, as if they were pesky flies, tossing them back into the air as they came at her one by one. Ivy, who appeared to be the strongest Shadow Girl, knocked her down with a hard kick to the back, but Salena stood up immediately, spread her wings, bared her fangs, and prepared to retaliate.

Lucy spied Edge cowering behind a rocky outcropping as the fight ensued; he didn't suspect that Aluna was approaching him from behind. She placed her two glowing peace fingers over his head and within seconds, Edge began to grow blonde hair—no fur—on his face and hands. His nose grew longer and became black on the end, while his ears, which were oversized before, grew larger and taller and then flopped over. Edge had morphed into a dog-boy. He barked and wagged his tail.

Scarlet, who stood a good distance away from Salena, was speaking in Vishphixie, as she held a palm full of red dust in front of her. Scarlet took in a deep breath and began to blow the colored dirt on Salena. Salena screamed and fanned her wings as if they were on fire. Whatever Scarlet had done appeared to hurt, and now Salena was infuriated.

"Hey, look over here," Opal screamed, and she tossed a bright yellow dust in Salena's face as she turned toward her.

"I'll kill you all!" Salena screamed, waving her arms around in front of her, as if she had been blinded.

That's when Lucy noticed that Salena had dropped the talisman in the struggle. It lay on the ground, right next to her pointy-toed boot and a tiny field mouse that scurried out of danger.

"Stay here," Lucy said to Jax and jumped into the air, hovering above the fight, ready to drop down and snatch up the Xietu before Salena discovered that it was missing.

But before Lucy could get close enough, she heard someone say, "Xiekallory!" It was Snow, perched on a high crystal peak. Lucy noticed that she was also staring at the Xietu.

The Xietu slowly began rising into the air. Salena swiped her arms wildly, clearly still unable to see the Xietu or that the Shadow girls had begun to fly in circles around her. They appeared to be wrapping her in something, because she began to struggle as if she were being caught in a web. But Salena was still too strong to be contained, and as she flailed her arms, she caught the velvet cord of the floating talisman by the tips of her grey skinned fingers.

Lucy flew straight for the talisman, grabbed hold of the lavender cord and yanking hard to pull it away from Salena. The antique cord ripped, sending the sparkling Xietu and the fate of Xiemoon spinning into the air.

Black feathers skimmed Lucy's fingertips as a bald-headed vulture snatched the Xietu in its curved beak and dropped into the dark forest of trees below her.

"Lucy, stop! She's escaped!" Snow called out.

Lucy looked beneath her to see VamPixies and Shadow Girls, Edge and Jax all looking up at her. Salena was definitely gone. Lucy floated down to the ground. "What happened?"

"I saw Salena use her Formling abilities. Just before she lost touch with the Xietu, she formed into that vulture,"

Snow explained. "Now we'll never find her…at least not until she wants to be found."

The Shadow Girls, the VamPixies and Jax gathered around Lucy, along with Edge, who followed his master—Aluna. She patted his head and said, "Sit. Good dog."

"Maybe you could find her, Lucy…with your Mind Sight," Ivy said.

"How can I do that?" Lucy wondered. "I have to wait until my Mind Sight tells me what to do. I can't control it. It just happens to me."

"Charlotte did," Scarlet said. "She mastered it."

Ivy said, "You come from a line of very strong women. Charlotte defeated Salena once before, and you can to."

"And we'll help you," Aluna said.

Snow, put her hands on Lucy's shoulders and said, "Xiemoon's fate is in your hands Lucy. You have to trust yourself and your ability."

Jax looked at Lucy. "Lucy, if anyone can do it, you can."

Opal added, "We have faith in you Lucy."

"Even if I could find her, I don't know how I am supposed to pry the Xietu out of her hands. She's a psychopath and dangerous! I know that you guys think I am something special, but I'm not. I'm just a regular girl," Lucy said.

She felt her throat tighten and tears welling up in her eyes. Before they fell in front of her friends, she rushed away and sat down alone, on the edge of the crystal mountainside. She needed to hear her own thoughts, without everyone telling her what to do or how she had a duty to save them. The truth was, she was afraid— afraid that Salena might kill her, afraid to disappoint everyone again, and afraid that she really wasn't anything special at all. She was just Lucy from Crystal Creek, and she wanted to go home.

Lucy wished she could disappear and become one of the tiny stars that filled up the sky around her. She sighed as one star twinkled with lunar light and then fell. She wished that she were stargazing from her own bed as she looked out over the Xiemoon valley. The dark forest below her glistened with dew as mist skimmed the earth and settled over the flowering fields that surrounded VamPixie Castle, far away in the distance.

She breathed in the night air and focused her gaze upon the giant moon that hung heavy above her. The moon calmed Lucy somehow. Her tears soon dried and her breathing quieted. She closed her eyes and listened to the insects chirp and the night birds coo. She began to feel warm, as if the moon's light was penetrating her whole body. Lucy felt safe.

The night sounds soon faded and Lucy's own doubt-filled voice was replaced by a faint whisper. Lucy didn't recognize this voice, and it didn't speak words that she could understand. It merely made sounds that were pleasing to her, even though they had no apparent meaning. Lucy did not move, but stayed there on her mountainside perch, all wrapped up in a blanket of light, and listened to the moon.

When she opened her eyes, it was not the moon in her view, but a vision of Salena's filthy fingers holding the Xietu. Salena kissed the Seizerstone and smiled. Then she slid under the rose-covered trellis and through the secret door to The Outside.

Salena turned back, as if she was talking directly to Lucy, and said, "Come to me Lucy. I'm waiting for you."

24

"I have to do this alone," Lucy said calmly, looking into the faces of each VamPixie, Shadow Girl, Moonsprite, and mortal around her.

"You can't go alone!" Jax protested. "I'll come with you."

"No. I can do this," Lucy said. And this time, she believed it. "Stay with them until I return."

"Be careful, Lucy," Opal said, as she hugged her. "And come back safe."

Everyone gathered around Lucy to say goodbye before she set off to find Salena on The Outside. Edge, who was still following Aluna around like a needy puppy, threw his arms around Lucy and licked her cheek.

"Yuck! Get him off of me," Lucy said.

Aluna curled her finger at Edge. "Bad dog," she said, and pointed to the ground beside her. "Stay!"

Lucy climbed on top of a giant crystal cluster of stones, spread her glistening wings and sprung off of Xienite Mountain's peak, soaring into the stars. She soon landed in the tall grasses, at the edge of Xiemoon and removed the jeweled key from around her neck. As she turned it in the lock, she felt like she was ready for anything. Her whole body tingled with energy and fearless strength.

But as Lucy stepped through the door to The Outside, her lavender wings disappeared, just as her little pink training wings had done each time she had crossed over in her dreams. "Honorary," she whispered to herself. She forgot that this would happen. She had also forgotten that she was actually just a mere mortal, an average girl, without wings, magical abilities, or super-human strength. She was not a VamPixie on The Outside.

Powerless and alone in the dark forest, Lucy stood completely still, all the bravery sucked out of her with the loss of her glittery appendages. How can I do this as ordinary Lucy? I don't have a chance against Salena, she thought. On top of her super-cruel personality, she has the talisman, which makes her even more wicked.

Her body felt heavy as she struggled to lift her feet off the ground. It was as if she were walking in water with cement shoes. She managed to lift one foot and drop it back into the crunchy fallen leaves, but this was all she could manage. As hard as she tried, she couldn't move a muscle. Lucy had lost her glow, and every ounce of strength she had. She tried to scream, but no sound came out of her mouth. Lucy looked up for the only thing that might be able to release her from this concrete body that she was stuck in, but even the moon had deserted her. All she saw were clouds.

From behind her left ear, she felt something tickle her neck. Then it moved to the right ear and whispered, "Stupid girl."

Salena, who had become the miniaturized version of herself, buzzed around in front of Lucy's face and said, "Hello! It's so nice to have you all to myself to chat. We have so much to catch up on, Charlotte."

I'm not Charlotte, you freak, Lucy yelled in her mind. She would have screamed it if she could have, but instead, she silently stared at the sky and waited for the moon to show herself. And then she remembered what Salu had told her; if the moon was not visible, she could imagine it to make her Mind Sight come. Lucy closed her eyes and conjured up a brightly shining moon in her mind. Slowly, her body began to soften, just as it always did when her visions started. Lucy held her body stiff, so Salena wouldn't know that she had been freed from her frozen position.

Under Lucy's closed eyes she saw Salu and Salena, who looked like a nicer version of her current mean self, with a very old man that Lucy did not know. Could this be their father? Then the man formed into a little grey mouse.

"Charlotte, you stole my heritage," Salena accused, disrupting Lucy's vision.

Lucy opened her eyes and saw Salena at the end of her nose. She tried not to cringe at the smell of Salena's foul breath as she spoke. For such a small person, it was extremely potent. It smelled like something had died in there.

Meanwhile, some kind of bug or creature had started to stir in the hood of Lucy's sweatshirt. Despite her desire to wiggle and slap whatever was crawling on her, Lucy remained completely motionless as she felt the thing's hairy body tickle inside the neck of her shirt and crawl down her shirtsleeve. Lucy held her breath until it slipped out from under the ribbed cuff of her sweatshirt and stopped on the back of her hand. She squinted to see the tiniest grey mouse she had ever seen.

Lucy wasn't sure what her Mind Sight meant, but she was certain that this ultra mini-mouse was important.

"And now it's time for me to take it back!" Salena said.

But Salena's final threat was thwarted as Lucy lifted her hand up between them, and asked, "Do you know this mouse?"

Salena's tiny jaw dropped open. "Papa!" Salena called out, darting in to try and snatch up the miniscule creature.

At first, Lucy wasn't sure what her Mind Sight meant, but when she heard Salena call the mouse 'Papa,' she knew that this mouse was pretty important to her.

"No you don't!" Lucy said, as she covered the mouse with her other hand and pulled it away. "Trade!" she demanded.

Salena's evil face contorted as she backed away and hovered in the air.

"I'll squash him!" Lucy said.

"No!" Salena screamed and flew in closer. "I'll kill you!"

"Go ahead, I don't care. I want to be immortal,"

Salena scowled back at her opponent.

"Give me the Xietu, and I'll give you Papa," Lucy said, holding Mouse out for view once again.

"No!"

"I told you, I'll squash him flat," Lucy threatened.

Pulling the miniature Xietu from her pocket, Salena held it in both hands and admired what she was about to give up. She looked at Papa mouse and back to her Xietu several times.

Lucy's heart raced as she stared intently at the small, but evil, Salena, hoping that she could find enough love in her cold little heart to save Papa mouse, and put aside her desire for revenge long enough to fork over the talisman.

"Oh wait, I think I hear Papa saying something," Lucy said, as she held the mouse up to her ear.

"What does he say?" Salena asked in a strangely girlish way.

"He says that he wants you to give me the Xietu and to save him. He says that the Xietu holds no power any longer because Salu destroyed hers. She burned her Xietu and without the other half of the Seizerstone, its power is lost.

"Liar!" Salena screamed.

"I'm not lying! Papa said it. If you don't believe me, ask him for yourself."

Salena flew off into trees.

Where did she go? Lucy didn't know if Salena had formed into another creature, or where she had gone. She looked around, scanning the trees for her crimson wings. With Salena out of sight, anything could happen.

"I'm going to kill Papa!" Lucy screamed. Her voice quivered. "Now!"

Salena appeared out of nowhere, buzzed up to Lucy, and held the tiny talisman to her chest. She snarled at Lucy, her fangs showing under her wrinkled lip.

Lucy held the mouse between her closed palms and pretended that she was about to smash the helpless creature between them. She and Salena stared at each other for what felt like hours to Lucy. Finally, Salena swooped in closer and held the Xietu out for the taking.

"Okay," Salena said.

"Me first," Lucy said, and reached for the Xietu. In Lucy's possession, the talisman magically grew to its mortal size, the Seizerstone glittering brightly in the center of its eye.

Salena seized Papa in her skinny grey hand, buzzed over to a nearby tree stump, and inspected him before shoving him into her pocket and zipping back to Lucy. "I can still make you suffer!"

The door to Xiemoon was just behind them. Clutching the silver pendant, Lucy turned and sprinted toward the archway of twinkling lights. But something had wrapped around Lucy's feet and she slammed to the ground, tangled and then bound tightly with what felt like an invisible rope. Lucy tried to kick off whatever held her ankles, but Salena was on her way, screaming with satisfaction for having captured her so easily. Lucy held the Xietu out in front of her like a shield and screamed, "Go Away!"

Salena's red wings sparked and then burst into flames. Her tiny body dropped to the earth below. Smoke billowed up from her wings.

"Did I kill her?" Lucy asked herself out loud. Destroying a VamPixie's wings seemed to be the only way to end their life. She had merely been trying to use the Xietu symbol for protection; she had no idea that this would happen.

The invisible ropes were no longer binding her legs. Lucy quickly stood up and crept over to the moss covered rocks where Salena was lying on her back, eyes closed, body limp. Lucy bent over the dead little Pixie. She is dead, Lucy thought. Then Salena opened her eyes and smiled weakly.

Lucy's entire body filled with horror.

"I'm not dead yet," Salena coughed.

Salena pulled Papa Mouse from her pocket and kissed his tiny little nose lovingly. "I love you, Papa." She smiled and kissed him again. "You would do anything for me, wouldn't you, Papa?"

At that moment, Lucy almost felt sad for Salena, who was obviously saying goodbye to her father—the field mouse—before she died. Again.

"You would even save my life!" Salena cried out and opened her mouth wide. Then she sank her razor sharp fangs into her Papa's back and sucked the life right out of him. "Mmmm," she purred, as his blood trickled down her chin.

Lucy gasped as Salena's charred wings immediately healed over, bringing her immortal body back to life and returning her wings to their slick, blood-red color. Lucy knew that without the healing touch of another VamPixie,

Salena would have died. But she didn't know that the blood of a living thing could save her life.

"Goodbye…for now!" Salena said, and she zipped away, disappearing into thin air.

With the Xietu in her possession and Salena out of sight, Lucy approached the door to Xiemoon. It was finally over and it was time to return the talisman. She pushed her hand against the invisible door that separated her two lives, but it seemed to be locked. That's strange, Lucy thought, and glanced down at the shiny Xietu in her opposite hand. The talisman should have allowed her to pass through without a key.

Lucy pulled her VamPixie key over her head and struggled to turn it in the lock. "It's jammed," she whispered. She removed the key, reinserted it, and attempted to turn it, but again, the lock still wouldn't release.

She slammed her body weight hard against the invisible barrier, but this too proved hopeless. She was too weak. Remembering that she still had one sugar bean cube in her pocket, leftover from before she left VamPixie Castle, Lucy retrieved it and put it in her mouth. Maybe this would give he the glow she needed to bust open the door. No glow, nothing but a tasty treat.

Have I been locked out of Xiemoon, she wondered? Did Salena do this?

She stood back, concentrated her will on opening the door and said, "Xiekallory!" She must have said it a million times with as much conviction as she could muster. But even with the magical Xietu in her hands, her own magical powers were useless on The Outside.

Lucy sat down on the damp earth, and leaned against a tree. "Forget it, you're not a VamPixie anymore."

Lucy looked up again toward the moon, hoping to invoke her Mind Sight for answers. But no answers came. There was no Mind Sight on demand. Even the moon had failed her.

Teary eyed, Lucy had no other choice, but to take her Xietu home.

The sky dawned on the walk down the familiar wooded path toward her house. Lucy walked numbly through the back door, past the laundry room where Scratch should have been sleeping, but wasn't, and up to her bedroom, skipping the creaky step as usual. Sleep came quickly for Lucy, the Xietu safely hidden under her pillow.

Soon enough, the sun shone brightly through Lucy's window. But she did not want to get out of bed. Lucy pulled the covers over her head to hide from the light.

It was the sound of the big pink nurse saying, "You get to go home today, you lucky girl!" that finally woke her.

25

"**What?** Where am I?" Lucy mumbled as she forced her eyes to open.

Mara sung out, "Wucy!" as she toddled through the hospital room door with Lucy's mom close behind her.

"Good morning sleepyhead! Ready to get out this place? Miss Jinny just has to sign your release papers, and we can take you home," her mom said, looking at the pastel clad woman on the other side of Lucy's bed.

Lucy took a deep breath and tried not to show that she was shocked to have woken up in the hospital bed that she left so long ago. Shouldn't she be at home in her own bed? Then she remembered that she had fallen asleep after talking with her Aunt Christine, and then she dream hopped

her way back to Xiemoon. So much had happened since then, but it seemed that nobody even knew that she was gone. Did she dream that she killed fire-breathing dragons and won the Xietu from Salena, or was she dreaming right now? Were the VamPixies and Xiemoon even real? Lucy thought that she had it all figured out before, but now, she doubted everything.

Lucy rubbed her eyes, cleared her throat, and asked, "Can I have a drink of water please?"

"Here Honey, I brought you some clothes to wear home, and here's your glasses. Do you want to go change?" Lucy's mom asked.

Lucy took the bag of clothes that her mother had packed for her into the bathroom. She tried not to breathe too deeply because there was an overwhelming smell of pine trees and bleach when she opened the door. Lucy put on her glasses, untied her hospital gown and looked over her shoulder into the mirror. She hoped to see a scar or a mark on her back that would prove that VamPixie wings had once grown there. But her skin was as clear and as perfect as ever. If her wings had truly been real, there would surely have been evidence that they had existed, wouldn't there? Lucy faced herself in the mirror. She was just as ordinary as she had been two weeks ago, before all this happened. Lucy's throat tightened as she pulled on her jeans.

Dressed and ready to get out of there, Lucy plopped down willingly in the unnecessary wheel chair that the nurse had provided for her patient.

"Let's go home," Lucy said. "Come on, Mara."

Mara climbed into Lucy's lap, and her mom wheeled the girls down the long grey hallway toward the exit sign. Lucy hugged her little sister tightly.

Some relief came when she saw Scratch waiting for her in the front seat of the car. His little black and white head poked out of the half opened window. When Lucy opened the door, Scratch bathed her in kisses, as if he hadn't seen her in weeks. "I'm so glad to see you, Scratch," Lucy giggled, as she wiped her face and got into the front seat.

The drive home was quiet, aside from Mara jabbering in the back seat and her mom repeating how happy she was to be taking her daughter home.

Strumming her fingers against the armrest, Lucy wondered where the Xietu talisman might be, and if she would ever be allowed back into Xiemoon. Or maybe the VamPixies and Xiemoon had all been a figment of her imagination in the first place. She felt as if she had been dropped into a labyrinth, and each time she thought she had found the way out, it turned out that she landed at another dead end. She stroked Scratch's back, as he lay curled up in her lap, and decided not to think about it.

"It's good to be home," Lucy sighed, as she walked up the front porch steps. The screen door creaked loudly as she pulled it open. There was something about the old family cottage that, despite it being old and in disrepair, it made her feel good. As she walked inside, Lucy could have sworn she heard a voice say, "You are safe here." She shook her head in disbelief and headed for the staircase to her room.

Her mom put Mara down next to the toy box and called to Lucy, "I'll make you some chicken soup for lunch, okay?"

"Sure," Lucy said, walking up the steps.

She closed the door behind her, and went straight to the pillow on her bed. She lifted the pillow and there it was— the Xietu. She had stashed it there after she took it from Salena, before she woke back up in the hospital. This was good. It proved that she wasn't crazy.

But then where was Salena? Even if the Xietu would protect Lucy from harm, it wouldn't stop Salena from trying to steal it from her, or from terrorizing the VamPixies, or even her family. Lucy worried that without her wings, strength, or magic to help her, Salena would eventually steal the Xietu back. For all she knew, Salena was lurking about, just waiting to get her alone in the forest again. And next time, she might actually succeed in killing her.

Lucy felt vulnerable and weak. The only power she had on The Outside was her Mind Sight, and although it had been useful, it didn't feel like the kind of strength she needed to fend off Salena and get back to Xiemoon with the Xietu. Lucy wondered if maybe her gift could be even more than what she had experienced so far. She had learned to access her Mind Sight when the moon wasn't visible by imagining it in her mind, and she had learned to listen to the moon and did her best to interpret her guidance.

So far, Lucy's Mind Sight told her what she needed to know. But Lucy wondered what might happen if she could ask the moon questions. Would the moon answer her?

Sitting cross-legged on her bed, Lucy gazed out the window into the moonless, sunlit sky, and closed her eyes. She started her moon meditation by visualizing a full moon, and thinking about what she wanted to know. Where is Salena? How do I open the door to Xiemoon? Will you help me get there safely? But Lucy was only confusing herself, and she wasn't Seeing anything at all. She sighed and opened her eyes.

The aqua blue air outside slowly changed to pink, faded into dusky purple, and finally to an indigo night. Her room was dark, aside from the muted light that was cast off by the waning moon. Lucy was entranced once again, feeling as if nothing else existed between her mind and the moon.

Because Lucy was controlling her visions this time, her Mind Sight felt a little different. First there was the familiar tingle behind her eyes, but then the prickly feeling crept down her back and over her entire body. Lucy imagined herself as she was, sitting on her bed, but in this time vision of herself she had her VamPixie wings. She saw them twinkling in the moonlight, and then she felt her wings flutter. Lucy felt goose bumps erupt over her body and the power she once felt as magical Lucy poured back into her body. Not only could she see herself as a VamPixie, she could feel herself become one.

Lucy's mom knocked on her bedroom door. "Lucy, are you all right? Your lunch is getting cold," she said and cracked open the door.

Lucy shoved the talisman under her pillow and fell back on her bed, whisking the covers overhead, making certain that the patchwork quilt was hiding every last sparkle of her VamPixie wings.

"Are you sure you feel okay?

Lucy heard the door creak open. She swallowed and used her best acting skills to conceal the truth. "I'm fine. I was just napping," she said from under the blanket.

"I made you some chicken soup," her mom said. "You can come down and get it when you're ready."

The door creak again and then closed. Lucy reached under her head for the Xietu, grabbed it, and sat up. From the top drawer of her bedside table, Lucy selected a lavender hair ribbon that she intended to replace the broken cord that once made the talisman a necklace. She pushed the ribbon through the hole, tied a double knot in the two ends, and slipped it around her neck.

Her jeweled wings lifted and vibrated with life. Now that she had them, she wondered how she would hide them from her mom. But her thoughts were interrupted by a knock at her bedroom door. Lucy lay back down, pushing her wings under the covers.

"Come in."

"Hey, how's it going?" Jax asked, throwing open her bedroom door.

"Okay, I guess," Lucy responded.

Jax stood there blankly. Lucy scanned his face for any sign that he might know about Xiemoon, but Jax didn't act like he had a clue that anything strange was going on.

"When did you get back?" Lucy asked.

Jax said, "Huh?" He looked confused.

"Oh, no. They memory erased you again," Lucy said from her bed. "Do you remember when I told you about Xiemoon?"

"Key-moon?" Jax said, raising his palms. He looked truly mystified.

Lucy shook her head and sighed. "Never mind."

"Do you want to watch a movie or something?" he asked. "But I don't want to watch anything about vampires." Jax stared at Lucy for a few seconds and then burst into laughter.

"You're such a jerk!" Lucy sat up in her bed, exposing her wings. "Look!" She couldn't help but smile.

"Hey, how did you do that? I thought your wings disappeared when you left Xiemoon?"

"Well they did, but I visualized them, and somehow I made it real with my Mind Sight. Well, at least it worked this time. Now I have to make them disappear before Mom sees me," Lucy said. "Watch this!"

Jax folded his arms over his chest and waited as Lucy looked intently out her bedroom window toward the empty sky. Again, the sky darkened briefly for her eyes and the moon appeared.

Jax gasped and said, "Whoa, your eyes are all sparkly! What's happening to you?"

Lucy did not answer or move for several minutes. Finally, her wings dissolved into dust and fell to her bedroom floor, leaving a trail of glitter around her feet.

"That was awesome!"

Lucy smiled with accomplishment, made certain that her Xietu was hidden under her t-shirt and followed Jax downstairs to the living room to watch movies. They spent the afternoon laughing at comedies. Even her mom and Mara joined them, with popcorn and blankets to keep cozy. Lucy realized how much she had missed her family while she was away in Xiemoon. And it helped keep her mind off Salena.

That night, Lucy smiled as she closed her eyes and snuggled into her very own bed, with Scratch burrowed in beside her, his wings illuminating the quilt from beneath. Lucy craved uninterrupted sleep. Salena, the Xietu, and any further dangerous adventures in Xiemoon could wait for tomorrow. She didn't want her Mind Sight to disturb her on this night. She was tired.

Before she drifted off, Lucy thought about Charlotte. There was still so much she wanted to know about her great grandmother. Lucy wished that she could have met her, and heard her tell her own stories of Xiemoon.

But that night, Lucy heard a voice whisper her to sleep. Although she had never heard Charlotte speak, she knew that the wise voice belonged to her great grandmother. She said, "Your wings have always been a part of you, and their power is in you, wherever you are."

And then Lucy dreamed the loveliest dream of all.

With that giant lavender full moon above her, and a ring of glittery red roses crowning her head, Lucy stood in the center of the circle. All the Xie tribes—the VamPixies, Shadow Girls, Moonsprites, and many others that she had not yet met, surrounded her. The Xietu hung over her simple dress, and her jeweled wings framed her beaming face. Salu, Scarlet, Snow, Opal, and Aluna, were in front of her. Jax was at her side, and Scratch sat at her feet.

White rose petals rained down over Lucy, drifting slowly to her bare feet. She breathed in the clean scent of lavender as each of her friends sprinkled her with the fragrant flowers. Salu sang the VamPixie Promise in Vishphixie, reminding Lucy that she was about to become a part of something ancient and pure. Lucy made her promise in English.

Friends forever, we stick together,
As sisters of the night.
With pure hearts and healing hands,
There will be no bloody bite.
Peaceful guardians of Xiemoon,
We promise to do right.
And listen to the wise Moon,
She is our guiding light.
VamPixies Forever!

"Lucy, the Xie people are honored to have you as our lifelong friend, as well as an honored VamPixie in the service of peacekeeping in Xiemoon," Salu declared. "Xiemoon will always be your second home."

Salu, Snow, Scarlet, Aluna and Opal pointed their electric peace fingers at Lucy. She felt the warm, big-hearted love of her friends, as their pink light covered her in a glowing dome of energy.

She felt alive and strong and brave.

Made in the USA
Lexington, KY
27 January 2012